James Hadley Chase and The Murder Room

》》 This title is part of The Murder Room, our series dedicated to making available out-of-print or hard-to-find titles by classic crime writers.

Crime fiction has always held up a mirror to society. The Victorians were fascinated by sensational murder and the emerging science of detection; now we are obsessed with the forensic detail of violent death. And no other genre has so captivated and enthralled readers.

Vast troves of classic crime writing have for a long time been unavailable to all but the most dedicated frequenters of second-hand bookshops. The advent of digital publishing means that we are now able to bring you the backlists of a huge range of titles by classic and contemporary crime writers, some of which have been out of print for decades.

From the genteel amateur private eyes of the Golden Age and the femmes fatales of pulp fiction, to the morally ambiguous hard-boiled detectives of mid twentieth-century America and their descendants who walk our twenty-first century streets, The Murder Room has it all. **》》**

The Murder Room
Where Criminal Minds Meet

themurderroom.com

T0352508

James Hadley Chase (1906–1985)

Born René Brabazon Raymond in London, the son of a British colonel in the Indian Army, James Hadley Chase was educated at King's School in Rochester, Kent, and left home at the age of 18. He initially worked in book sales until, inspired by the rise of gangster culture during the Depression and by reading James M. Cain's *The Postman Always Rings Twice*, he wrote his first novel, *No Orchids for Miss Blandish*. Despite the American setting of many of his novels, Chase (like Peter Cheyney, another hugely successful British noir writer) never lived there, writing with the aid of maps and a slang dictionary. He had phenomenal success with the novel, which continued unabated throughout his entire career, spanning 45 years and nearly 90 novels. His work was published in dozens of languages and over thirty titles were adapted for film. He served in the RAF during World War II, where he also edited the RAF Journal. In 1956 he moved to France with his wife and son; they later moved to Switzerland, where Chase lived until his death in 1985.

By James Hadley Chase
(published in the Murder Room)

My Laugh Comes Last

James Hadley Chase

An Orion book

Copyright © Hervey Raymond 1977

The right of James Hadley Chase to be identified as the author of this work has been asserted in accordance with the Copyright, Designs and Patents Act 1988.

This edition published by
The Orion Publishing Group Ltd
Orion House
5 Upper St Martin's Lane
London WC2H 9EA

An Hachette UK company
A CIP catalogue record for this book is available from the British Library

ISBN 978 1 4719 0396 0

All characters and events in this publication are fictitious and any resemblance to real people, living or dead, is purely coincidental.

No part of this publication may be reproduced, stored in a retrieval system or transmitted in any form or by any means without the prior permission in writing of the publisher, nor be otherwise circulated in any form of binding or cover other than that in which it is published without a similar condition, including this condition, being imposed on the subsequent purchaser.

www.orionbooks.co.uk

1

Looking back, I can now see that the seeds of this nightmare that happened to me were sown some four years ago: seeds that finally produced blackmail, two murders and a suicide.

Four years ago, I was a badly paid service mechanic, working for Business Equipment & Electronics. My father, who was their head accountant, got me the job. When I left school, he had suggested I should study electronics, and sent me to the local university where I got a Master's degree. While I was still at school, he also suggested I learned to play golf.

'More business is done on a golf course, Larry,' he said, 'than in a boardroom.'

I discovered I was a natural golfer, and later I became a fanatic about electronics.

All the week, including Saturdays, I humped a heavy tool bag, in the evenings I went to night school and studied electronics. Sundays, I played golf.

I had this arrangement with the golf pro at Creswell golf course that I could play a round for free every Sunday morning at 08.30, and in return, I would look after his shop until lunchtime. It was an arrangement that suited us both as I couldn't afford to become a member, and he could spend the morning out on the course.

On this hot June morning, I decided to concentrate on my putting, and not play a round. Looking back, this was an act of fate. If I hadn't decided to sharpen up my putting, I wouldn't have met Farrell Brannigan, and this nightmare wouldn't have happened to me.

I had just rolled in a twenty footer when a gravelly voice said, 'That's one hell of a putt.'

I turned round.

Standing on the edge of the green was a vast man around sixty years of age. He was over six feet tall, and nearly as wide. He had all the trappings of the very rich: his golfing outfit screamed money. His fleshy, sun-tanned face, his aggressive chin, his china-blue eyes told me he was important people.

'Can you repeat that, son?'

I stepped back, put another ball down, took a look at the cup, now thirty feet away, then giving the ball plenty of top spin. I sent it on its way. Knowing the lie of the green backwards, I knew the ball would drop, and it did.

'Jesus! Mind if I try?'

'Go ahead, sir.'

He fiddled around as most bad golfers do, then aiming at the cup, he stabbed, and was five feet short.

'I'm doing that all the time,' he moaned. 'There must be some trick in this.'

'There is, sir.'

He regarded me.

'Okay, you tell me. What do I do wrong?'

'For one thing, your putter is too short for you. For another, you looked up when you struck the ball. For another, you were standing all wrong.'

'My putter tooshort? Damn it! I've played …' He paused, then went on. 'What sort of putter should I use?'

'I can fix that for you, sir.'

'Go ahead and fix it.'

I took him to the pro's shop, opened up and sold him a putter that was right for his height. Then I took him back to the putting green and explained how to read the lie of the green. This was something he knew nothing about. After an hour, I was getting him to roll them in in three putts instead of five. He was delighted.

'I have another problem, son,' he said. 'You just might fix it. I have a hell of a hook.'

'Suppose we go over to the driving range, sir?'

We went. He teed up, and just as he was shaping for his swing, I stopped him. I got his feet right and his overlap grip turned. He drove a nice one down the middle.

'Just keep your feet like that, and your grip as you have it now, sir, and you'll be fine.'

He hit three balls down the middle, then he beamed at me.

'I appreciate this, son,' he said. 'I have a match on this morning. I guess you are a lifesaver.'

'Glad to be of help, sir. I'll get back to my putting.'

'Hold it. What's your name?'

'Larry Lucas.'

'Glad to know you.' He thrust out his big hand. 'Farrell Brannigan.'

I did a double take. Farrell Brannigan's name was as well known as Gerald Ford's. He was the President of the Californian National Bank with branches through the state.

'My privilege, sir,' I said, as we shook hands.

He grinned, obviously pleased his name had impressed me.

'What's your line, Larry?'

'I'm a service mechanic with BE & C.'

'Is that right?' He regarded me. 'What do you know about computers?'

'I have a Master's Degree.'

'University?'

I told him the name of my university.

'Okay, Larry. Go back to your putting. Come and see me at the bank at ten tomorrow.' Then nodding, he picked up his driver and moved back to his tee.

Four years ago, this had been my great moment. I had a feeling that Brannigan was going to do something for me. Now, looking back, I can see I was taking my first steps into this nightmare.

On Monday morning at exactly 10.00, I was shown into a vast office with a vast desk between two vast windows with a panoramic view of the city.

Farrell Brannigan was rolling a golf ball along the floor, using the putter I had sold him.

'Come on in, Larry,' he said. 'I won that match, thanks to you.'

'Congratulations, sir.'

'This is a fine putter you sold me.' Putting the putter down, he moved to his desk, waved me to a chair and sat down. 'How are you fixed for next Sunday? How about playing a round with me? I'd like your ideas about my approach shots. How about it?'

I could scarcely believe my ears: to play golf with Farrell Brannigan!

'That would be fine with me, sir.'

'Okay. The wife likes me home for lunch. Suppose we meet at the club at eight o'clock. Right?'

'Yes, sir.'

'I talked to your Dean this morning. What the hell are you doing wasting your time as a service mechanic? According to the Dean, you're a top-class computer and electronic engineer: the best student he's ever had.'

4

'My father wanted me to stay with BE & C. He had a theory that it was better to be a big fish in a small pond than a little fish in a big pond. My father died a few months ago. I am now making plans. IBM have made me an offer.'

'How old are you?'

'Twenty-seven, sir.'

'What do you earn?'

I told him.

'Forget IBM,' he said. 'With your qualifications, son, you are handling your future career all wrong, but never mind. I'm going to fix that.' He paused to light a cigar, then went on. 'You know something Larry? When you get to my position, it's fun to play God. From time to time, I do it when someone does something for me. I haven't made a mistake, and I don't think I'm going to make a mistake with you. Ever heard of Sharnville?'

'Yes, sir.' My heart was beginning to thump. 'It's an up and coming town halfway between here and 'Frisco.'

'Right. We are opening a bank there. This bank is going to be something special as Sharnville, in a few years, is going to come on the map in a big way. I want the latest computers, the latest business machines and calculators that money can buy. Do you think you could outfit the bank?'

My heart was now slamming against my ribs.

'Yes, sir,' I said, trying to keep my voice steady.

He nodded.

'I'm going to give you the chance to do it. You have a little time. The bank doesn't open for six months. I'll give you three weeks to submit ideas and estimates. If they are not what I want, I'll try elsewhere. How about it?'

'That's fine with me, sir.'

He dug a big thumb into a press button and his secretary came in.

5

'Take Mr Lucas to Bill,' Brannigan said. He looked at me. 'Bill Dixon is my architect. You and he will work together.' As I got to my feet, he went on, 'See you Sunday,' and with a wide grin, a wave of his hand, he dismissed me.

I liked Bill Dixon on sight. He was a short, heavily built man with a wide, easy smile. In spite of a few grey hairs, he didn't look more than a few years older than myself.

'I've heard all about you,' he said, as we shook hands. 'So FB is playing God again.'

'That's what it looks like.'

'He played God with me. He had a flat in the pouring rain, and I stopped and changed the wheel. Now, I'm here.' He laughed. 'Do something for him, and he does something for you ... a great guy.' He raised a finger. 'But make no mistake about it: he's as tough as he is great. If you don't deliver, or if you step out of turn, you're out.'

He then told me about the bank.

'You'd better come with me to Sharnville and meet Alec Manson who is going to run the bank. Here's the blue-print. You'll see the setup. Your job will be to supply all the office equipment, and Manson will tell you what he wants. Suppose we meet at the Excelsior Hotel tomorrow at Sharnville?'

When I got back to my bedsitter, I studied the blueprints. This wasn't going to be a small bank. This was going to be a big, imposing bank. It ran to four storeys with underground vaults and safe deposit boxes.

This, I told myself, was a chance in lifetime. I felt completely confident I could handle it.

I remembered my father.

A big fish in a little pond or a small fish in a big pond. Why not a big fish in a big pond?

I made my decision.

I had some five thousand dollars in the bank. I could live on that for some months. If Brannigan turned down my suggestions, I could still make a living.

So I called BE & C and told the staff manager I was quitting. I didn't bother to listen to what he was saying. I just hung up on him.

There was no doubt that Sharnville was an up and coming town. Buildings and office blocks were going up everywhere.

I met Dixon at the Excelsior Hotel and he introduced me to Alec Manson, the future manager of the bank. He was in his early forties, tall, lean and remote, but we got along together. He seldom smiled, and didn't appear to have any other interest except banking.

'The ball's in your court, Mr Lucas,' he concluded after explaining the bank's requirements. 'We want the best, and it is up to you to provide the best.'

For the next four days, I didn't move from my bedsitter. I had all the data I needed. My landlady provided me with meals, and by Saturday night I had the estimates and my suggestions down on paper for Brannigan, and had worked out a possible future for myself, always providing Brannigan was satisfied.

The next morning I was waiting outside the golf pro's shop as Farrell Brannigan drove up in his Caddy.

'Hi, son,' he said, beaming at me. 'It's going to be a fine day.' He got his trolley and golf bag out of the trunk. 'Come on, let's get at it.'

The first nine holes developed into a golf lesson. Brannigan was eager to improve his game. He played off 18. His approach shots were pretty terrible as he was prone to under-club. I got that sorted out by the ninth hole. He was delighted with his driving and putting, it certainly had sharpened up. He suggested I gave him a stroke a hole, and we would play real golf.

I wanted him to win this match, so from time to time I deliberately fluffed shots, and as we approached the eighteenth we were level pegging. He had a four-footer to roll in and I a fifteen-footer. I could have made the putt, but again I deliberately fluffed it and overran by two feet.

'I think I've got you, son,' he said, beaming, then shaped up for his putt. He took his time, and I began to sweat he would miss but he didn't. The ball dropped, and he turned, grinning from ear to ear.

'The best goddamn game I've ever played. Let's go and get us a drink.'

I said all the right things, and he grinned even more.

Settled in a corner of the comfortable clubhouse bar, he ordered beers, lit a cigar, sat back and regarded me.

'How's it coming, Larry?'

'Subject to your approval, sir,' I said, 'I've got it tied. I have the estimates and the list of computers, machines, calculators and so on with me.'

'That's fast work. Let me see.'

I took out the typewritten sheets and handed them to him. He went rapidly through the estimates, puffing at his cigar. I waited, sweating, until he reached the final sheet which told him what it would all cost. He didn't bat an eyelid.

'This looks fine, son,' he said.

'I think I should tell you, sir, I quit BE & C last Monday. I'm now working on my own,' I said.

He regarded me, and looked at the estimates again, then grinned.

'What it amounts to, son, is you're planning to handle this deal yourself and collect commission on everything you sell us.'

'That is correct, sir.'

'A big fish in a big pond, huh?'

'What you said about me wasting my time as a service mechanic struck a note.'

He laughed.

'I'll say.' He finished his beer and stood up. 'I've got to get back for lunch. Okay, Larry, leave this with me. We have a board tomorrow. I'll get my man to look this over, talk to Manson and then talk with my directors. Where can you be reached?'

'My address and telephone number are on the back of the estimate.'

'Thanks for the game ... best I've played.' Then nodding, he left me.

I got the green light from Dixon after three hellish days in my bedsitter, waiting to hear.

'You mean it's on?' I said, scarcely believing what he was saying.

'They've okayed everything. I have a letter signed by FB authorising you to buy on their behalf. Pick it up at my office tomorrow, and you're in business.' He paused, then went on, 'Congratulations, Larry.'

It took me four weeks of non-stop work to get the bank equipment. Farrell Brannigan's name acted as an open sesame. IBM, Apex and even BE & C fell over themselves to give me credit. I had no problems. My commission, once the deal was finished, would be impressive.

As soon as I had all the equipment for the bank ready for delivery, I moved to Sharnville. I took a two-room furnished apartment in a modest complex. Manson, Bill and I worked non-stop, and we made a good team.

One night, while Bill and I were sharing hamburgers together, he said, 'What do you know about electronic security, Larry?'

'What there is to know. I specialised in that at the university.'

'I think FB will let you install the security if you can convince him. He's rather like a big kid so make your ideas fancy. Really give him the works … money no object.'

So that was my next job. I got estimates, suggestions and consulted the top experts. By the time I was through and got my ideas on paper, I was sure I could give the bank the finest security gimmicks that could be put together.

Brannigan called me.

'Bill says you have security ideas, son. I'd like to hear about them. Let's play golf.'

After the game, and this time I didn't let him beat me, but made it a close run thing, we sat in the clubhouse bar and I told him about my ideas.

'Mr Brannigan,' I concluded, 'if you accept this equipment, I will guarantee you will never have security trouble. Your bank in Sharnville will be the safest bank in the world.'

He stared at me, and his face lit up.

'The safest bank in the world!' he exclaimed, then slammed his fist into the palm of his hand. 'The safest bank in the world! I like that. By God! I like that! We could use that as a slogan! The safest bank in the world! That's really something. We'll hit the headlines!' Then he paused and looked hard at me. 'That's no idle boast, son? If we advertised, and really went to town with a slogan like that, would it stand up?'

'Mr Brannigan,' I said quietly, 'Sharnville bank will be the safest bank in the world.'

'There's a board tomorrow. Come along and tell the story. I don't know a goddamn thing about electronics, but all you've told me sounds fine.'

So I went along to the bank's boardroom and gave ten stony-faced directors a presentation on how to make a bank secure. I produced gimmicks, blueprints and told them the cost.

They listened, and when I had finished FB nodded, gave me a broad grin and said I would be hearing from them.

As I left the boardroom, I heard his gravelly voice say, 'The safest bank in the world. Goddamn it! What a slogan!'

Three days later, Dixon telephoned me to tell me I had the green light.

'That must have been a great show you put on, Larry. They loved it. There is going to be worldwide publicity. The safest bank in the world! FB is having a ball.' He paused, then went on. 'You realise what this means, don't you? FB is planning to open other branches, and you will automatically get the equipment and the security jobs for all future branches, and I'll get the job of building them. I've been looking at the estimates. Your commission ...'

'I've already worked that out,' I said.

'Suppose we talk about this, Larry? You and I could work together. I've money too.'

So we talked about it. We agreed to become partners, but before we committed ourselves, we went along to Brannigan and told him what we had in mind. He liked the idea, and gave us his blessing which meant a lot. He said he would steer business our way. So we set up a firm to be called Better Electronics Corporation, and decided to make our headquarters in Sharnville. We rented a small office. We worked all day and half the night. We got a small, expert staff together.

11

After six months, the 'safest bank in the world' opened with a flourish with a world press coverage, TV cameras on the scene as important people arrived. The President of the United States looked in for a brief ten minutes, arriving on the roof of the bank in a helicopter. Nothing went wrong. FB and his board were happy.

From then on, Sharnville grew fast. I was there to supply the office equipment and security, and Dixon was there to build. We moved into bigger offices. Farrell Brannigan's name gave us the green light as more and more industrial corporations opened in Sharnville. The saying was: 'What's good enough for FB, is good enough for us.' We got all the business, and it was plenty.

So at the beginning of our fourth year, we moved to even bigger offices and employed a staff of fifty. We had become big fish in a big pond.

Although I worked nine hours a day at the office, and took work back to my apartment, I kept my Sundays free for golf. I joined the Country Club, and every first Sunday in the month, Brannigan drove up and we played golf. I had no trouble in finding a partner for the remaining Sundays. Everyone at the club was friendly, and playing golf with Brannigan gave me a status symbol.

But the seeds of disaster sown on that June Sunday four years ago had germinated, and during my four years of success, they grew fast into this nightmare of blackmail and murder.

On this Sunday, an equally hot June morning, the evil fruit was ripe to be picked. I was getting ready to leave for the golf course when Brannigan telephoned to say his car had broken down.

'God knows what's happened to the goddamn thing, but it won't start. I've called the garage, but it's Sunday. By the time I get someone up here, it'll be too late.'

I decided to play golf anyway and take pot luck in finding a partner. I arrived soon after 08.15, and asked the pro, not too hopefully, if anyone was wanting a game.

'There's a young lady on the putting green, Mr Lucas, who is looking for a game. She's a stranger here, but watch it!' He grinned. 'She looks like a golfer to me.'

That's how I met Glenda Marsh: a tall, slim redhead with big green eyes and a personality that was electric. She made a big impact on me as I introduced myself.

'Imagine!' she exclaimed as she shook hands: a good, firm grip. 'I was going to call on you tomorrow.' She went on to explain that she was a freelance photographer and was here to do a photographic reportage on Sharnville. 'I was told you are the electronic wonder man, and I hope to get shots of your setup and you.'

This was flattering when she told me she had been commissioned by *The Investor*, an important financial monthly with a big circulation.

Remembering I had a heavy programme for the following day, I said if she liked to come to my office at 18.00, I would be happy to see her. She said she would.

We played a round of golf together, and she was good. I had to work at it to beat her. As we played, I kept looking at her, and the more I looked, the more I liked what I saw. She was really some woman!

I had fooled around with a lot of girls, but during the past few years I had had no time for fooling. Now, not working under such pressure, I was ripe for a woman. I wondered about her as we walked side by side down the fairway. There was something about her that warned me she was no easy, casual lay. She had a 'hand-off' air about her that made her much more intriguing to me than any other girl I had known.

After the game, I suggested we went to the clubhouse for a drink, and I would introduce her to some of the important members, but she shook her head.

'Thank you, but I have a date. Thanks for the game, Mr Lucas. I'll see you tomorrow.' Smiling, she left me.

I watched her walk to her Mini-Minor. While I had been with her, this day had been in technicolour, now it turned to black and white as she drove away.

2

'That's it,' Glenda said, 'and thank you. I hope I haven't taken up too much of your time.'

She had arrived at my office at 18.00 and it was now 19.35. She had taken shots of our showroom, our small factory, with close-ups of our four engineers who smirked happily while they worked at their benches. She had taken some twenty shots of me at my desk. She had been efficient and impersonal, but now, as she put her Nikon into her camera bag, she relaxed and gave me that friendly, dazzling smile.

'No problem,' I said, getting to my feet. 'I had cleared my desk before you came. I hope you have what you want.'

'Not quite: I would like some personal information about you, but perhaps you would like to set up another date. I understand Farrell Brannigan gave you your start. I would like to hear about that. It would make a great story.'

'Suppose we go into that over dinner?' I said. There was something about her that hooked me. I wanted to keep her with me as long as I could. 'There's a place down the street that serves a decent meal.'

She nodded.

'Let's do that.'

After our game of golf, and after she had driven away, I had had her on my mind. Usually, I had a snack at the clubhouse and mixed with the other members, but this time, I wasn't in the mood, and had driven down to the beach, had a swim, then lay alone in the sun and had thought about her.

There is some mysterious chemistry that no one has yet explained that takes place when a certain man and a certain woman meet. Some call it love at first sight. Whatever it is, it is a sudden fusion, and, being an electronics man, I saw it as getting the right electrical connection and turning on the switch.

This had now happened to me. Glenda Marsh, at first sight, had become the woman I really wanted. Fate, destiny, call it what you like, had brought us together, and the switch, for me, had been turned on.

But had the turned-on switch done anything for her? Maybe her chemistry hadn't responded as mine had. This was something I had to find out.

I had walked with her to the Mirabeau restaurant where I often dined. She was one of those women who didn't dither when studying a menu. She took one brief glance, then said she would like a clam chowder. It was a good choice. I went along with it.

'Now tell me about yourself,' she said, resting her elbows on the table and regarding me with those big green eyes.

So I told her about my father, my golf, BE & C and Brannigan. We had nearly finished the meal by the time I had finished my life story.

'Are you married, Mr Lucas?'

'No.' I smiled at her. 'But as soon as the pressure is off, I want to get married.'

'Any particular girl?'

'There is a vague chance I have found one, but I'm not sure yet.'

She regarded me, then looked away. Her lips curled into a little smile. I had the idea she got the message.

While I was ordering coffee, she lit a cigarette, and when the waiter had gone, she said, 'A real success story, Mr Lucas. Congratulations.'

'It happens. I had the knowledge, but then I had luck.'

'But you had to have the knowledge. Tell me … is it a fact that the Sharnville bank is the safest in the world or is that just a publicity stunt?'

'It is the safest bank in the world. I should know: I installed all the security equipment … it is no publicity stunt.'

She looked impressed.

'It would make a great news story. Tell me about it.'

'Sorry, that's not for me to talk about. Before I got the job, I had to sign a paper not to talk. If you want the story, talk to Alec Manson who runs the bank, but I don't think he will tell you much. The bank's security is top secret.'

'Well, I can try.' She smiled her dazzling smile. 'Would you give me an introduction to Mr Manson?'

'No problem. Now, tell me something about yourself. Where are you staying in Sharnville, and how long will you be here?'

'At the Excelsior, and I'll be here at least a month.'

'Do you like the Excelsior?'

She grimaced. 'Does anyone like staying in a hotel?'

'Would a two-room furnished apartment with a kitchen interest you?'

Her green eyes sparkled.

'Would it not! That would be marvellous!'

'Then I can fix it for you. There's an empty apartment in my complex. I can fix it for you to have for a month.' I signalled for the bill … 'Like to see it?'

'Why, thank you, Mr Lucas.'

17

I looked directly into the big green eyes.

'Make it Larry, Glenda,' I said. 'We are going to be neighbours. My apartment is across the corridor.'

The following morning, she had moved into the apartment. I called Alec Manson and told him about her, explaining she was doing a reportage on Sharnville for *The Investor*, and she would like to talk to him.

In his dry, clipped voice, he said she could come any time, so I called Glenda and told her to go ahead, and if she had nothing better to do, why not let us have dinner together this evening?

This time I took her to a sea food restaurant. While driving her along the coast road, I asked how she made out with Manson.

She raised her slim hands and let them drop, in her lap.

'Like interviewing an oyster. He allowed me to shoot the outside of the bank and the lobby. When I asked him about the security, he stayed dumb. I have no story, Larry.'

'I warned you. After all, Glenda, if he let you into the secrets of the bank security, it would no longer be the safest bank in the world, would it?'

She laughed.

'You have a point, but what a story!' She looked at me. 'But you can tell me.'

'I could, but I won't. Brannigan has plans to open four more banks along the coast, and I get the security job. I want that contract. Brannigan is a very smart cookie. He would know at once I had been talking. Sorry, Glenda.'

'Oh, well!' She shrugged.

We arrived at the restaurant and settled at our table. After consulting the menu, we both settled for lobsters.

While waiting, she asked. 'What is crime like in Sharnville?'

'That's something I know nothing about. You talk to Sheriff Joe Thomson. He'll be glad to give you a rundown. I play golf with him from time to time. He's a smart cookie.'

While we were eating, I thought it time to get to know something about her personal life.

'You've quizzed me, Glenda. It's my turn. Are you married?' I asked this question with trepidation.

'Yes ... it didn't work out.' She pulled a little face. 'I'm a working woman. He was an auto salesman. He just sat around and did nothing. I made a mistake.'

'We all make them.'

'I guess.' She looked at me and smiled. 'But I'll confess, I get tired sometimes of this job: it's all race and chase: living in hotels, motels. It pays off, but ...' She shrugged.

'Ever thought of trying marriage again?' I asked, looking directly at her.

She stiffened, and those green eyes lost their sparkle.

'There is nothing to stop anyone thinking, is there?' She pushed her plate aside. 'That was good.'

'Coffee?'

She nodded.

There was a long pause as we both regarded the ocean, shimmering in the moonlight. I longed to rush it, but knew it would be a mistake. I wanted to tell her I loved her. I wanted to tell her I had lots of money, could give her a home and wanted her to be with me for the rest of my life, but I told myself I had to wait to get some sign from her. I had to be patient. I had a month.

Back at my complex, we rode up in the elevator to the tenth floor, and we paused outside the door.

'Thank you, Larry. It has been a lovely evening.'

'Let's do it again tomorrow night.'

She regarded me thoughtfully, then shook her head.

'No. Come and have dinner with me. I'll cook for you.' Then she smiled. 'It's odd how people meet.' She put her hand on my arm. 'Tomorrow at eight,' and leaning forward, she brushed my cheek with her lips, smiled and disappeared into her apartment, gently shutting the door.

I stood for a long moment, staring at the door, knowing now our chemistry had fused, and scarcely believing it.

We sat side by side on the settee. The single lamp cast shadows. We had eaten the best meal I had ever had: crab soup, and the breasts of duck in rice with soya sauce. We had had three large gin martinis each, and had shared a bottle of Beaujolais. I had never felt more relaxed nor more contented.

Very softly, Bing Crosby sang *The Blue of the Night* from a cassette she had put on.

Having her by my side, the atmosphere, that golden voice singing, the food and the drink was my moment of truth. I felt I couldn't ever be so happy, so relaxed. This was a memory to hold on to and remember.

I didn't want to talk, I didn't want her to talk. I just wanted to sit there, slightly drunk, listening to that voice, looking at her as she lay back, her eyes closed, the shadows from the lamp, making her face even more beautiful than it was.

The song came to an end, and there was a sudden emptiness in this rather shabby, but comfortable room.

She opened her eyes and smiled at me.

'Everything finally comes to an end.' She reached out and switched off the recorder.

'That was marvellous,' I said. 'The meal was marvellous.' I looked at her. 'You are marvellous.'

She reached for a cigarette, lit it, then lay back, but away from me.

'Last night, you asked me if I ever thought of trying marriage again. I want you to know about Alex, my husband.'

My mind came to attention.

'Your ex-husband?'

'I'm still married to him.'

My feeling of utter relaxation left me. I sat up and stared at her.

'You are still married to him? I thought you were divorced.'

'I wish I was.' She stared at the burning ember of her cigarette. 'God! How I wish I was!'

'But why not?' I was now leaning forward, my hands into fists. 'What's the problem?'

'You don't know Alex. With him, there is always a problem. He won't give me a divorce.'

'I don't understand, Glenda. Did he leave you or did you leave him?'

'I left him. I couldn't stand him any longer. He's not interested in women. He isn't interested in anything except money and himself.'

'When did you leave him?'

'About six months ago.'

'There must be some way you can get rid of him.'

She shrugged.

'I can buy him off. For twenty thousand dollars, he will give me a divorce. It is as shabby and as sordid as that.'

'You mean for twenty thousand dollars you can be free of him?'

'Why talk about it?' She moved impatiently and flicked ash into the ashtray. 'I wanted you to know, Larry, because I'm falling in love with you.' She put her hand on mine. 'I thought I could go through life alone, but now I have met you, my ideas have changed. It's odd, rather frightening, how a woman meets a man, then something happens. This must be our last meeting, Larry, and I mean that. I know you have money, and I know you love me, but I will not be bought!' She looked directly at me. 'You are not to say you will give Alex the money to free me. That would be unacceptable to me! I am working and saving. In another two years, I hope to pay him off, but I won't have you waiting all that time.'

'I'll lend you the money, Glenda! I won't give it to you. I'll lend it, and when you can, you can pay me back.'

'No!' She stood up. 'It is getting late.'

I got to my feet and put my arms around her and pulled her against me.

'Yes,' she said, her face against mine. 'Just this once, Larry. I long for you.' Her body pressed against mine.

Then the front door bell rang.

The sound of the bell was like an electric shock. We jerked apart and both looked towards the front door which opened directly into the living-room.

'Don't answer it,' I whispered.

'I have to.' She gestured towards the uncurtained window. 'Whoever it is knows I'm here.'

'I'll get out of sight.' I was in a panic, and this needs explaining. I was now regarded in Sharnville as one of their leading citizens. I was on equal terms with all the big shots of the Country Club. To be caught in the apartment of a married woman photographer would cause a buzz of gossip that would tarnish my present image.

'No!' she said curtly.

Stiff with apprehension, my heart thumping, I watched her cross to open the front door.

The last man I wanted to see stood in the doorway: Sheriff Joe Thomson.

As I had told Glenda, I had often played golf with Thomson. We got along well enough together, but talking to him as we walked the fairways, I came to realise this man was a dedicated cop. He was around forty-five years of age; tall, lean, tough, and had been in police business for some twenty years. He had the face of a hungry eagle: small cop eyes, a hooked nose and paper-thin lips. When playing golf, he seemed relaxed, but there was no humour in him. He took golf seriously, and I had the impression he could be utterly ruthless when the chips were down.

He looked into the dimly lit room. His small eyes rested on me, and his eyebrows shot up. Then he looked at the dining table with the unmistakable evidence that Glenda and I had been eating together.

He took off his Stetson hat.

'I apologise, Mrs Marsh, for this late call. Seeing your light on, I thought I'd drop in and give you the data of our crime record as you wanted it so urgently.' Then raising his hand, he saluted me. 'Hi, citizen.'

'Hello there, Joe,' I said, my voice husky.

'How kind of you, Sheriff,' Glenda said, completely at ease. 'Do come in. Mr Lucas is just leaving. He has been telling me interesting stories about Sharnville.'

'Is that right?' The cop eyes went to me, then back to her. 'Larry certainly knows this town. You could call him a founder member. I won't come in. My lady has dinner waiting for me.' He offered an envelope. 'You'll find all the dope here, Mrs Marsh. If you want any further information, you know where to find me.' He waved to me. 'See you, citizen,' then putting on his Stetson, he walked away to the elevator.

Facing each other, we stood motionless until we heard the elevator doors shut, then we looked at each other.

The spell had been broken.

Not three minutes ago, I had been aching to make love to her, and she had been aching for me, but not now.

'I must go,' I said, my voice unsteady. 'He keeps a finger on the pulse of this town. We'll have to be much more careful from now on, Glenda.'

She lifted her hands in a gesture of despair and let them drop.

'For a moment I thought ...' She turned away. 'Nothing ever works out for me ... nothing!'

'If Brannigan or Manson or the Mayor thought I was fooling around with a married woman, Glenda, I would be in trouble, and so would my business. I have a partner to consider. I just must be careful!'

She gave a little shiver, then turning, she looked at me.

'Fooling around? Is that what you call it?'

'Glenda! Of course I don't! But they would think so.'

She forced a smile.

'Don't look so worried. I told you this is the last time. I promise you I won't spoil your success story.' The bitterness in her voice was like the flick of a whip, but I had to go. I was sure Thomson would sit in his car to make certain I did leave.

'I'll contact you, Glenda. We just have to be more careful.' I moved towards her, but she stepped back, shaking her head. 'Glenda! We must work this out! I love you, but you must understand I just can't take chances.'

'I do understand.' Again the forced smile. 'Goodbye, Larry,' and leaving me, she went into her bedroom and shut the door.

At this moment, all I could think of was Thomson, sitting in his car, waiting to see if the light in my apartment went up. I hurried across the corridor, unlocked my front door and entered. Without turning on the lights, I went to the window and looked cautiously down on the street. His car was still there, I turned on the lights, then taking my time, so he could see me, I slowly drew the curtains.

He started his car and drove away.

Two days later, while I was coping with the morning's mail, Bill Dixon breezed into my office. I hadn't seen him for the past week. He had been working on a building project some fifty miles outside Sharnville.

'Hi, Bill,' I said. 'When did you blow in?'

'Last night.' He dumped his heavy briefcase on the floor and sat down, facing me. 'I called you, but you were out.'

I had been down to the beach, alone, trying to figure out what to do about Glenda. I knew I was in a tricky situation. After pacing the floor of my living-room on the night we had parted and hearing her voice, saying *I long for you*, going over and over in my mind, I had thrown caution aside, and had crossed the corridor and rung her bell. The time then had been 01.30. She didn't open the door. I rang again, then I heard the elevator coming up, and scared, I retreated to my apartment. The following morning before leaving for the office, I again rang her bell, and again she didn't answer. In the office, as soon as I had got rid of the mail, I telephoned her. There was no answer. By lunchtime, after trying to get her again, I was fit to be tied. I had to talk to her! But we had to talk where no prying eyes could see us. If she had been divorced, there would have been no problem, but I kept thinking that maybe her husband was having her watched, and if he cited me as the other man, this would badly dent my image in Sharnville and the business Bill and I had built up would take a financial knock. This sounds crazy in these modern days, but I knew Sharnville: leading citizens were expected to behave themselves, and I was now a leading citizen.

I tried to contact her in the evening, and again the next day, without success. I went down to the garage and found her car gone. I wondered, with a sick, sinking feeling, if she had left Sharnville, and I would never see her again.

That evening, I went down to the beach and considered what I should do. She was the one woman for me. I now knew that. I was even prepared to wait two years if I had to, to marry her, but not if I could find some much quicker solution. After thinking, I decided I would have to find out more about her husband. It seemed to me that if I could meet and talk to him, offer him money, without Glenda knowing, he would be willing to free her. To me, she was worth far more than money. Although the bulk of my money was tied up in the business, I knew it would be no problem to get twenty thousand dollars from Manson on loan.

Finally, I decided I had to talk to her, and somehow, get her husband's address from her. But where was she? Where had she gone?

On this morning, as I parked my car outside the office block, I saw Sheriff Thomson striding along the sidewalk.

He paused and nodded to me.

'Hi, citizen.' This was his usual greeting to all his friends.

'Hello there.'

'That's a smart young woman you sent to me ... Mrs Marsh.' He regarded me with his cop eyes. 'I reckon the articles she's going to write won't do Sharnville any harm.'

I forced a grin.

'That's why I suggested she should talk to you.'

'Yeah.'

There was a pause, then I said casually, 'She's doing a reportage on my business, Joe. This is important to me. I've got some more information for her, but I can't contact her.'

He pushed his Stetson hat to the back of his head.

'She's out of town right now, but she'll be back. She told me she's doing a piece on Grimmon's store, and she's got herself invited to old man Grimmon's place in LA.' He stared thoughtfully at me. 'She'll be back. She wants to get photos of the jail.' He scowled at a motorist who was about to double park. Seeing him, the motorist drove on. 'How about a game of golf next Sunday?'

'I'd like to, Joe, but this Sunday I'm playing with Mr Brannigan.'

He nodded.

'Mr Brannigan, huh? I heard you play golf with him. You sure move in the top circles.'

I tried to laugh it off.

'Strictly between you and me, Joe, he plays with me because I coach him. I've got his handicap down from eighteen to twelve.'

He straightened his hat, wiped the end of his nose with the back of his hand, then nodded.

'You've got business. I've got business. See you,' and he walked on.

So Glenda was in Los Angeles. She hadn't run away from Sharnville! I would have a chance to talk to her on her return!

'We've won the contract, Larry,' Bill said, beaming. 'It's a beaut! I reckon it will be worth at least a hundred thousand to us!'

For the next two hours we went over the contract to build a factory to produce furniture elements. Bill had the heaviest work of designing the factory and building it. My share of the project was to provide typewriters, calculators and photocopy machines and get them installed.

When we were through, Bill sat back and regarded me.

'Pretty good, huh? We're growing fast, but we need more capital. We'll have to carry this firm for six months before we get their money. Right now, they are asking for credit, but they are sound.'

'I'm playing golf with FB Sunday. I'll talk to him. He'll give us credit.'

Then out of the blue, he asked quietly, 'Who is Glenda Marsh?'

If he had reached across the desk and poked me in the jaw I couldn't have been more shaken. I gaped at him.

'Glenda Marsh,' he repeated, his voice now sharp.

I got hold of myself.

'Yes ... Glenda Marsh. She arrived here this week. She is doing a reportage on Sharnville for *The Investor*. She's already covered our setup.' I realised I was talking too fast, and I made the effort and slowed down. 'She wants your side of the story, and to take photographs. She's already talked to Manson and Thomson and she's interviewing Grimmon right now. She's doing this reportage in depth. It'll do us a lot of good.'

'That's fine.' He hesitated, then went on, 'Look, Larry, we are partners. We have now got off the pad. We are in big business. Sharnville is rather special. Although it is growing fast, it is still small minded.'

I felt a chill run up my back.

'I'm not with you, Bill.'

'Let me spell it out. After trying to contact you last night I went to the Excelsior bar for a snack and a drink. The bar was buzzing about you and this Marsh woman. Fred Maclain was full of booze. As deputy sheriff, he has his ear to the ground. He was saying you had taken this woman out to dinner twice, and Sheriff Thomson had found you in her apartment late at night. Maclain says she is married and is trying to get a divorce. She volunteered this information to Thomson. Certain citizens here are now thinking there is something going on between this woman and you. In a couple of days, the whole town will be buzzing.'

This was the time to have told him I was in love with Glenda, but, stupidly, I didn't.

'For God's sake!' I said. 'I did take her out twice to dinner because I wanted her to get the complete picture of what you and I have done. There was more talk to be done, and she suggested we talked in her apartment and she would give me dinner. In this small-minded town, now you tell me, that was a mistake, but we talked business all the time.'

He relaxed and grinned at me.

'That's good news, Larry. Hearing all the talk, I began to wonder if you had hot pants for this woman. As a favour, and as your partner, in the future, will you be more careful?'

'There's no favour about this, Bill! Okay, I admit I didn't think, but it never crossed my mind that these people could start gossiping. Mrs Marsh is doing us a favour, getting us into *The Investor*. What's wrong in taking her out to dinner?'

'Nothing. The slip-up, Larry, was having dinner in her apartment.'

'Yes ... that was stupid of me, but I didn't think.' I forced a grin. 'It won't happen again.'

He studied his fingernails for a long moment, then looked directly at me.

'When I need a woman, I have someone in 'Frisco. I've made sure there is no blowback. Sharnville is different. You and I are under a spotlight. For God's sake, be careful!'

'There's nothing to be careful about!' I said angrily. 'This is just malicious gossip.'

'Yeah, but gossip could give us lots of trouble.' He ran his fingers through his short hair. 'I don't have to remind you we rely on Brannigan. We are expanding fast, and he is backing us. Because of his say-so, we have this big loan. Without it, Larry, expanding as we are doing, we could go bust. Now here's something you might not know. Brannigan is a Quaker. I told you when we first met, he was great, but take a wrong step, and you would be out. Some years ago, he had a secretary who really slaved for him. He thought she was the tops. Then she got snarled up with a married man, gossip started, and Brannigan threw her out. It didn't matter to him that she had been the best secretary he ever had. The fact she committed adultery made her a leper to him. He seems to have this thing: men or women fooling around with married women or men are strictly out. So for both our sakes, Larry, keep away from Glenda Marsh. If Brannigan gets a whiff of this, he could call our loan, and we would be sunk.'

'There's nothing going on, Bill,' I lied. 'Okay, I made a mistake. Relax ... it won't happen again.'

He grinned.

'Fine. Now I want you on the site tomorrow. These people are staying in 'Frisco, and it would be a smart idea for both of us to stay in their hotel and finalise the deal. How about it?'

I hesitated. I would have liked to be here when Glenda returned. Then seeing Bill's inquiring stare, I nodded.

'Okay, Bill. I'll get my desk cleared. Tomorrow then ...'

When he had gone to his office, I sat staring out of the window. The writing was on the wall, but I wanted Glenda. I wanted her as I had never wanted any other woman. I had to talk to her! I had to convince her that I loved her, and she meant everything to me. I was sure I could persuade her to let me buy her husband off. Once this was done, and she got her divorce, there would be no problem, and I was sure Brannigan, once he knew I was marrying her, would raise no objections.

But how to contact her? I now had to spend a couple of days in 'Frisco. She would be returning to Sharnville, probably tomorrow. I didn't want her to think I had gone away to avoid her.

For some time, I wrestled with this problem, then I did the stupidest thing I have ever done. I reached for a sheet of notepaper and wrote to her.

Dearest Glenda,

I have to go to 'Frisco for a couple of days. I have tried to contact you, so I write.

I must talk to you: please don't refuse me. Already there is gossip about us. Please be understanding about this. We must talk. I am sure we can fix this problem. Will you meet me on Sunday at eight o'clock a.m. at Ferris Point? It is about four miles from Sharnville and will be deserted at that time. We can then discuss our future without prying eyes.

Take the highway towards 'Frisco, then turn at the fifth intersection on your left. This will bring you to Ferris Point.

If you love me, as I love you, you will come.

Larry.

I put this letter in an envelope, and when I returned to my apartment that evening, I pushed the envelope under her door.

Ferris Point is a tiny bay, hedged in by sand shrubs and sand dunes, and offers perfect swimming. I often went there when I wanted to be alone. Sharnville as yet hadn't discovered it.

I drove down the sandy, uneven road to the bay, and leaving my car under the shade of a tree, I made my way through the sand shrubs and on to the stretch of golden sand.

Would she come?

I had had two hectic, but profitable days in 'Frisco. The deal had gone through, but we would need yet another loan from the bank. I was confident we would get it, and I told Bill I would talk to Brannigan this day while we played golf.

But first Glenda.

Then I saw her.

She was sitting on the sand, wearing an emerald-green bikini, her knees up to her chin, her hands gripping her ankles, the sun reflected on her red hair.

I stopped and looked at her, and at this moment I thought she was the most desirable, wonderful woman on earth.

She looked towards me and smiled.

As I joined her, she said quietly, 'So you see, Larry, the temptation was too great. All my good intentions of not seeing you again ...' She grimaced. 'I have had you on my mind, night and day.' She released her ankles and dropped back, stretching out. 'Don't let's talk, darling ... let's make love.'

I threw off my shirt and slacks and she got rid of her bikini. I knelt over her, loving the sight of her body, wanting to kiss every inch of her.

'No ... quickly, Larry. Come into me.'

There was an urgency in her voice that set me on fire. As I covered her and she guided me into her, she gave a soft cry. Her legs wrapped around me. Her fingers dug into my flesh.

The sun, the sound of the sea and the rustle of the leaves made a perfect background as, feverishly, we reached the climax. Her fingers moved down my back, holding me in her.

'Again,' she gasped. 'Please ... again!'

Then a voice from nowhere said, 'Break it up, you sonofabitch,' and a shoe thudded into my ribs. The kick was so violent, it threw me off her. Rolling on my back, I stared up.

A short, squat man was standing over me. I saw him as a nightmare, sharply in focus: bearded, suntanned, eyes like currants stuck in honey bread. A panama hat was pulled down, shading his bushy eyebrows. He wore a crumpled, dirty white suit.

As Glenda struggled to her feet, he hit her with the back of his hand, a vicious blow that sent her sprawling.

A murderous rage swept through me. I launched myself at him, my hands groping for his throat. We smashed down on the sand, and for a long moment, we fought like animals. His strength was horrifying. Although I had a grip on his throat, he broke my hold. His fist smashed into my face, his knee came up into my groin. The hot sun suddenly turned dim as if there was a sudden eclipse. I clung on to his coat, and again his fist smashed into my face. Still this murderous rage gave me strength to throw him off. As he fell on his back, I heaved myself up and using both fists, I clubbed down on his face. My body was screaming with pain, but I didn't care. All I wanted now was to kill him. As I raised my fists to club him again, a light exploded inside my head, and the sun snapped off like a fused light.

I swam out of unconsciousness, feeling the grit of sand on my skin. I moved, and a blinding flash of pain shot through my head. I heard myself groan. I lay still. My groin ached. My ribs ached. My face ached.

The sun burned down on me. I could hear the gentle lap of the sea on the beach, and the rustle of leaves in the breeze.

Very slowly, I gathered myself together. Very slowly, my hand holding my head, I sat up. I rode the pain, hammering inside my skull, forced open my eyes and stared around the deserted beach.

No Glenda. No squat man. I had Ferris Point to myself.

I waited, my hands holding my head, then I became aware that my hands were sticky, and with a shudder, I took them from my head and looked at them. They were red with drying blood.

Because every movement I made sent pangs of pain through me, I remained staring down at my blood-stained hand, motionless.

Maybe twenty minutes crawled by before my brain became activated.

Where was Glenda? What had happened?

I looked at my watch. The time now was 08.45. I had been unconscious for some thirty minutes. Making an effort, I struggled to my feet. The sea and the beach swirled around me, and I had to sit down again. I waited. Then I again made the effort, and this time, swaying like a drunk, I managed to stay upright.

The pain in my head raged. I set off slowly: each step as if I were wearing divers' boots, until I reached the sea. Kneeling, I washed the blood off my hands and scooped salt water against my aching face. The salt stung, but the sting brought me alive. I got to my feet and looked up and down the empty beach, then plodded back to my clothes.

It took me some time to dress. Twice, I had to sit down and rest, but finally I got dressed, and by now I felt more or less alive.

34

What had happened? Where was Glenda? Where was the squat man in the crumpled white suit?

As if in a nightmare, I trudged across the hot sand to where I had left my car. I opened the door and sank thankfully into the driving seat. I tilted the driving mirror and stared at myself. My right eye was puffy and black. The right side of my face was swollen, green and red, where the squat man had hit me.

Then in spite of my raging headache, my brain became more active. In two hours' time, I was due to play golf with Brannigan, and while we played, I had to ask him to extend our credit. That was out. I had to telephone him and cancel our game. That was the first thing I must do. Then Glenda ... but Brannigan first.

I drove away from Ferris Point. There was a café-bar at the top of the sand road and I slowed, then again looking at myself in the driving mirror, I realised I would cause a sensation if I went in there to use their telephone, so I drove on.

I was lucky with the traffic which was light at this time. My head screamed at me, my face continued to swell. If a traffic cop had spotted me during the four miles back to my apartment, he would have stopped me, but no traffic cop appeared.

I scarcely knew what I was doing by the time I drove into the underground garage. I staggered out of my car, and looked at the bay where Glenda kept her car. It was empty.

Five minutes later, I was somehow talking to Brannigan. I caught him as he was leaving for Sharnville. I told him I had had a car accident and would he excuse me?

'Are you hurt, son?' he asked, concern in his voice.

'My face and my windshield had an argument. I'm all right. I just have to nurse my bruises.'

'What happened?'

'Some lunatic. I took evasive action and banged my face.'

'That's too bad. Anything I can do?'

'Thanks, no. I'll be all right. Sorry about the game.'

'We'll set up another date. Take it easy son,' and he hung up.

My head still raging, I crossed the corridor and rang Glenda's bell.

'She's gone, Mr Lucas.'

I turned slowly. The old black cleaning woman was at the end of the corridor with her mop and her bucket.

'Gone?'

'Sure, Mr Lucas. She left around seven this morning. She seemed in an awful hurry, carrying her bags. I offered to help her, but she walked through me as if I wasn't there.' She gaped at me. 'Your poor face, Mr Lucas!'

'I had a car accident,' I said and retu. ned to my apartment.

I dropped on my bed and held my aching head in my hands. What was happening? What the hell was happening?

Forcing myself upright, I went into the kitchen and got ice from the refrigerator. I wrapped ice cubes in a towel and held the towel to the back of my head. Moving slowly, I returned to the living-room, holding the ice bag against my head. It helped a lot. Then after some minutes, I transferred the ice bag to my swollen face. That also helped. The raging pain began to diminish.

Then the telephone bell rang.

Glenda?

I snatched up the receiver.

'Mr Lucas?' A brisk male voice.

'Who is this?' I managed to mumble, shifting the ice bag to the back of my head.

'The name is Edwin Klaus.' He spelt out. 'K-l-a-u-s.' A pause, then he went on, 'We have business together. I'll be with you in ten minutes, Mr Lucas, but first do me a favour. Take a look in your car trunk. I am sure you have a headache, but make the effort. Take a look,' and he hung up.

A hoax call? A nut?

I sat still. No, not a hoax call. A cold chill swept over me. I dragged myself upright and walked slowly to the elevator. I rode down to the garage. I reached my car and unlocked the trunk. I swung up the lid.

Curled up, like an obscene foetus, blood on his crumpled white suit, his beard matted with blood, was the squat man.

His blank eyes gazed up at me as only dead eyes can gaze.

3

As I opened the door to my apartment and walked unsteadily into my living-room, I saw him, sitting in my favourite armchair, his legs crossed, his hands resting in his lap, relaxed and at ease.

He could have been anything from fifty-five to sixty-five years of age. His thick, snow-white hair was immaculate. Everything about him was immaculate: his charcoal-grey suit, his white silk shirt, the Pierre Cardin tie and the glistening black shoes. His face could have been chiselled out of teak: nut·brown, a thin beaky nose, a slit for a mouth, big slate-grey eyes and flat pointed ears.

The shock of finding the squat man dead in my trunk had stunned me. I felt as if I were experiencing a horrible nightmare, and in a few moments, I would wake up and find, to my utter relief, all this had never happened, and it was just another Sunday morning.

This man, sitting facing me, was just an addition to this nightmare. I closed the door and leaned against it and stared at him.

'I found your door open,' he said. 'Excuse me for taking the liberty. The name is Edwin Klaus: K-l-a-u-s.'

I felt a trickle of sweat run down my aching cheek. This was no nightmare: this was for real.

'What do you want?'

His slate-grey eyes, as expressionless as blobs of ice, regarded me.

'I want to help you.' He waved to a chair. 'I can see you are suffering. I told Benny to be careful.' He lifted small, brown hands in a gesture of resignation. 'He doesn't know his own strength. Do sit down, Mr Lucas.'

Because my head began to ache again, and my legs felt shaky, I moved to the chair and sat down.

'You have a problem, Mr Lucas. It would seem you too didn't know your own strength,' Klaus said in a soft, gentle voice. 'But your problem can be arranged if you care to accept my help.'

'Who are you?' I asked, staring at him.

'We won't go into that for the moment. The problem is Alex Marsh, whom you murdered. What are you going to do about the body, Mr Lucas?'

I closed my eyes. The scene came back to me. I had wanted to kill him. I remembered smashing my fists down on his up-turned face. I was lifting my fists to hit him again when I received a blow on my head. I had hurt him: probably broken his nose, but I was sure I hadn't killed him. If only this pain in my head would go away so I could think clearly!

'I didn't kill him,' I said, meeting Edwin Klaus' slate-grey eyes.

'That is for the judge and jury to decide, isn't it, Mr Lucas?'

I got to my feet and, moving unsteadily, I went into the bathroom and swallowed four Aspro tablets. I ran the water, then picking up a sponge, I bathed my face. I was now beginning to think more clearly.

I didn't know who this immaculately dressed man was, but my instinct told me he was a blackmailer. I put my hands on the toilet basin and forced myself to stand upright. I stared at my reflection in the mirror above the toilet basin. I stared at a stranger: someone remotely resembling myself, but with a puffy bruised cheek and wild, frightened eyes. I remained staring for some five minutes, and then the pills began to work, and the pain in my head began to recede to a dull throb.

Alex Marsh! So the squat man had been Glenda's husband!

Who was this man, sitting in my living-room so quiet, so relaxed, offering to help me?

I waited, still holding on to the toilet basin, still staring at myself in the mirror until the throb in my head became bearable. He had asked me what I was going to do with the body in the trunk of my car.

What was I going to do?

My immediate thought was to call Sheriff Thomson and let him handle the whole thing. If I did, would he, would anyone, believe my story? Suppose, by the merest chance, I was believed, I knew I would be finished in Sharnville. I would have to admit I had been making love to a married woman when her husband surprised us. Would they believe someone – who? – had hit me over the head while her husband and I were fighting?

I thought of the body, screwed up in the trunk of my car,.For a moment I had the wild idea of driving the car to some isolated spot, dragging the body out and burying it. A wild idea! This, I knew, I couldn't do.

Your problem can be arranged if you care to accept my help.

Why should this man offer to help me? What was in it for him? This I had to find out.

Now in more control of myself, I returned to the living-room.

Edwin Klaus was still sitting in my favourite armchair, relaxed, his legs crossed, his hands in his lap. He exuded infinite patience.

'Feeling better, Mr Lucas?' he asked. 'I don't want to hurry you, but, no doubt, you have heard of rigor mortis. In an hour or so, Marsh will be very difficult to handle.'

I felt a cold shudder run through me. This, I hadn't thought of, but now began to think about it. Marsh had been forced into my trunk, curled up. His body could jam when he stiffened. The thought turned me sick.

I sat down, facing him.

'I didn't kill him,' I said. 'While we were fighting, someone hit me over the head. That someone must have killed him while I was unconscious.'

'Mr Lucas,' he said patiently, 'at the moment, it doesn't matter who killed him. The fact is that he is in the trunk of your car, and he can't remain there much longer. Do you want my help or don't you?'

'Who are you? Why are you offering to help me?'

'The name is Klaus: K-l-a-u-s.' He spelt it out. 'The reason why I am prepared to help you is that I have followed your career, and find it remarkable how well you have succeeded. I think it would be a tremendous pity for you to lose all you have built up and have worked for.'

'Don't tell me you are offering this help for nothing. What do you get in return?'

He lifted his small brown hands and let them drop back in his lap.

'Something, of course, but this we must discuss later. The immediate problem is the disposal of Marsh's body. I have an organisation that is equipped to handle this kind of emergency. However, you may not wish to accept my help. You can either call the Sheriff and face a certain murder charge or you can attempt to dispose of the body yourself. You have the freedom of choice, Mr Lucas. I assure you if you refuse my help, you will hear nothing further from me. It is entirely up to you.'

'What do you want from me? I must know!'

'A service, but I am not prepared to discuss this until later.'

'I must know! Do you imagine I'm that stupid I would do a deal with you without knowing what the deal is?' I said, raising my voice.

Again he lifted his small brown hands.

'Then I take it you don't want my help.' He got to his feet. 'Then I will leave you. You had better hurry, Mr Lucas. Very soon the body will be impossible to handle. Don't forget to buy a spade, though where you will get one on Sunday will be your problem. I suggest the safest way for you is to bury him at Ferris Point, but you must hurry. I wish you luck,' and he moved to the door.

My mind was working swiftly. While he was moving to the door, I visualised all the grinding hours of work to build Better Electronics. I thought of my position as one of the leading citizens of Sharnville. I thought of Bill Dixon. Then I thought of driving my car to Ferris Point, digging a grave, if I could find a spade, dragging the body from the trunk and dragging it to the grave. The very thought of touching that squat, blood-soaked body sent a sick chill through me.

I assure you if you refuse my help, and you attempt to dispose of the body yourself, you will hear nothing further from me.

It was just possible I would hear nothing further from him, but he had only to put an anonymous telephone call through to the Sheriff to fix me.

A service?

What did that mean? By now I was in such a turmoil, I didn't care.

'Wait,' I said feverishly.

I had to get rid of the body! I had to have his help! Once rid of the body, I would be in a better position to deal with this man. Once I knew what service he wanted, I would be able to think of a way to outwit him. I had to have time to think!

He paused at the door and looked at me.

'I agree. I need your help,' I said, my voice husky.

'Very wise, Mr Lucas.' He moved back to his chair and sat down. 'I have three trustworthy men who will handle it for you, but you must go with them. You must see what they intend to do so you are convinced that, once buried, the body will never be discovered. If you will go down to the garage, you will find them waiting. The whole operation can be over in an hour or so. I suggest you go now. The longer you wait, the more difficult the operation.'

I stared at him.

'And when do you pick up the price tag?'

'There's plenty of time for that. Let us get this problem solved first. Go along, Mr Lucas.' He glanced at his strap watch. 'I am already late for an appointment.'

Bracing myself, I left him and rode down in the elevator to the garage. The time was now 10.15: still a safe hour. The people who lived in my complex seldom stirred into life on Sunday before midday.

As I came out of the elevator, I saw them, standing by my car.

Three men.

As I approached them, I looked searchingly at them.

The man who caught my attention was leaning against the driver's door. He was tall, lean, around twenty-five years of age. He had blond hair and a beard. He had minor movie star good looks. His eyes, exuding a cocky confidence, were sky blue. He looked, from his heavy tan, as if he spent days idling in the sun, most certainly ogling the girls. He had on a green singlet and tight white jeans.

The second man was standing at the head of the car. He was built like a bar bouncer: dark, hairy, a flat face, little eyes and long black sideboards. As a muscle man for a B movie he was perfect. He wore a shabby leather windcheater and black slacks.

The third man was a negro. He was so tall, he was resting his elbows on the roof of the car. His massive shoulder muscles rippled under a white T-shirt. He reminded me of Joe Louis, when in his prime.

The bearded man came forward with a cocky, cheerful grin. 'I'm Harry, Mr Lucas,' he said. 'That's Benny,' he jerked his thumb at the second man. 'And that's Joe.'

The negro's face split into a dazzling grin, but the man called Benny just stared sullenly at me.

Benny! The man who had hit me over the head!

'Let's go, Mr Lucas,' Harry said. 'I'll drive. You just take it easy.'

The other two got into the back seats while Harry went around and opened the passenger's door for me. I wasn't fooled for one moment by this politeness. I felt the menace of these three men as one feels the oppressive atmosphere of an approaching thunderstorm.

I got in the car. Harry went around and slid under the driving wheel and drove the car up the ramp and on to Sharnville's main street.

Church bells were ringing and people were on the move. Harry swung the car down a side street, and keeping to the side streets, he headed for the highway. He drove just below the speed limit and drove well.

Joe, sitting behind me, began to play a harmonica. The tune he played was sad and forlorn. It could have been a negro spiritual.

As we headed towards Ferris Point, my mind was busy. I had an instinctive idea that Benny, after knocking me over the head, had been the one who had murdered Marsh. He had that sullen, brutal look of a man who would kill without thought or feeling. My head still ached, and my face hurt me. My mind wasn't clear enough yet to form a complete picture of what was happening to me. I felt as if I were still in a nightmare, but it was gradually dawning on me I was now in a deadly trap. By allowing Klaus to get rid of Marsh's body, I was delivering myself into his hands.

Harry swung the car off the highway and drove down the sandy road to Ferris Point. He pulled up under the shade of a clump of palm trees.

'Wait a moment, Mr Lucas,' he said. 'I'll take a look-see.'

He got out of the car and walked around the high-growing sand shrubs.

Joe stopped playing his harmonica. He and Benny got out of the car. I sat still and waited. After a few minutes, Harry returned.

'It's okay. Let's go, Mr Lucas. We have some digging to do.'

Joe opened the trunk of my car and produced two trenching tools. Leaving Benny by the car, Harry, Joe and I walked into the jungle of shrubs.

In sight of the deserted beach and the sea, Harry stopped.

'How about here, Mr Lucas? We'll put him in deep.'

I surveyed the place, looked around, and then down at the bare patch of sand, surrounded by shrubs.

'Yes,' I heard myself say.

Joe began to dig. It was heavy work. The sand kept falling back into the hole he was making. The sun, by now, was hot.

I stood there in my nightmare, waiting.

When Joe had made a seven-foot trench of about a foot deep, Harry, using his trenching tool, began to clear the sand Joe was throwing up. The work moved faster.

The two men were sweating. I watched Joe's muscles rippling, and the sweat dripping from Harry's beard. The whole scene was so unreal, I could have been doing a moon walk.

When the trench was some five feet deep, Harry said, 'Okay, Joe. Hold it.'

Joe grinned, wiped the sweat off his face with the back of his hand and climbed out of the trench.

Harry turned and looked at me.

'Well now, Mr Lucas, this is your funeral, isn't it? We want another foot deeper.' He offered me his trenching tool. 'Do some digging!' The sudden vicious snap in his voice told me I had no alternative. I took off my jacket, took the trenching tool and stepped down into the trench.

Harry and Joe moved back.

Still in this nightmare, I began to dig. I had only dug for two or three minutes, when Harry said, 'Fine, Mr Lucas. Joe'll finish it. He digs digging,' and he laughed. He reached down, caught hold of my wrist and pulled me out of the trench. Joe took my place, and in a few minutes, the trench was some six feet deep.

'Do you think that's okay, Mr Lucas?' Harry asked. 'I can't see any child or dog digging down that far. Once he's in there, he's in for good. What do you say?'

I draped my jacket over my shoulders, sweat streaming down my aching face.

46

'Yes.'

Harry looked at Joe.

'Go get him.'

The negro ran off towards the car.

I waited.

Harry, holding the trenching tool by its blade, stared at the beach and the sea.

'A nice spot,' he said. 'I wouldn't mind being buried here. Better than those crummy cemeteries with their crosses and flowers.'

I didn't say anything.

Joe and Benny appeared, carrying the body of the squat man. I turned away, feeling sick. I heard a thump as they dropped the body by the open grave.

'Mr Lucas, just take a look. Make sure, huh?' Harry said.

I turned.

Joe and Benny moved back. There was the squat man, bloody, and in death, lying on the sand.

Harry gave me a sudden hard shove, and I staggered forward so I was right on top of the body. I looked down in horror. His face had been smashed in. I could see the white of his brains on his broken forehead.

'Okay, Mr Lucas,' Harry said, coming forward and taking hold of my arm. 'Let's get back to the car. Benny and Joe will fix him. You happy? I want you to be happy about this.'

I jerked away from him and walked unsteadily back to my car. He kept by my side. When we reached the car, his hand again took hold of my arm and he steered me firmly to the back of the car. He opened the trunk.

'Here's a mess, Mr Lucas, but don't worry your brains. We'll fix it for you.'

I looked at the blood-soaked rubber lining of the trunk and turned away.

'Get in the car and relax, Mr Lucas. You don't have a thing now to worry about.'

I opened the car door and sat in the passenger's seat. Marsh's smashed, bloody face swam in my dazed mind. I sat there until Joe and Benny returned. They got in the car. Harry slid under the driving wheel.

'I'll drop you off at your place, Mr Lucas,' he said, 'then Joe'll fix the car. I'll have it put back in your garage this afternoon. You don't have a goddamn thing to worry about.'

Not a thing, I thought, until Edwin Klaus comes around to pick up the price tag.

I spent the rest of this Sunday in my apartment, holding an ice bag to my face and considering my position.

I was sure Klaus intended to blackmail me. But how strong was his position? The body had been buried. No one saw Glenda nor myself at Ferris Point. At least, I saw no one on the drive down and on the beach. Suppose I told Klaus to go to hell when he came to pick up the price tag? What would he do? It seemed to me that by arranging to bury the body, his blackmail teeth were drawn. Suppose he called the Sheriff and told him where to find the body and implicated me? What proof had he I had murdered Marsh? I had only to keep my nerve and deny everything to be, in what seemed to me at the moment, a strong position.

I realised that my story to Brannigan of a car accident to account for my bruised face was dangerous. Every car accident, no matter how trivial, had to be reported to the Sharnville police. They were very strict about this. I would have to think of a better story than a car accident, and finally, after some thought, I came up with a better story. My mind then shifted to Glenda. Was she involved in this? Loving her as I did, I tried hard not to think she had been the bait on the hook. There was one way to find out. Although it was Sunday, I felt sure *The Investor* worked around the clock. I reached for the telephone and asked the operator to connect me with New York. I said I wanted to talk to *The Investor*'s office. After a delay, I got through. I asked to speak to the acting editor. There was more delay, then a brisk voice said, 'Harrison. Who is this?'

'I'm sorry to bother you, Mr Harrison,' I said, 'but it is a matter of urgency that I contact Mrs Glenda Marsh who I understand freelances for you.'

He repeated the name, then said, 'You are in error. We don't know anyone of that name, and we don't employ freelances.'

'Thank you,' I said, and hung up.

I got up and walked into the kitchen and wrung out the towel, then I wrapped more ice cubes and returned to my armchair. I had an empty void inside me. So Glenda had been the bait on the hook. Was she still in Sharnville? I doubted it. Surely this put me in a stronger position to tell Klaus to go to hell. If he now tried to involve me, I could not only involve him, but also Glenda, and maybe, once the Sheriff began to question her, she would tell the truth. I found it hard to believe that she didn't love me.

By 16.00, the swelling in my face had gone down. I now only had a black bruise on my cheek. My head ceased to throb. I was feeling jaded but more confident that I could deal with Klaus if and when he tried to put on the screws.

Remembering my car, I went down to the garage.

My car stood in the bay. It had been washed and polished. After a moment's hesitation, I opened the trunk. It was immaculate with a new rubber mat: no blood, no sand, no body.

As I was closing the trunk, Fred Jebson, who lived below me, drove in.

Jebson, an accountant, was one of those hearty, garrulous men who always liked to chat up anyone in sight.

'Hi there, Larry,' he said, getting out of his car. 'Didn't see you at the club.' Then he stared at me. 'For Pete's sake, did he catch you with his wife?' And he gave a bellow of laughter.

I felt my insides shrink, but I forced a smile.

'I had an argument with a golf ball,' I said. I took a No. 5 down to the beach. The ball ricocheted off a tree and caught me before I could duck.'

'Jesus!' He looked concerned as he stared at me. 'You could have lost an eye.'

'I guess I was lucky.'

'You can say that again. I've got some great stuff for a bruise like that. Come on up, Larry. I'll give it to you. My kid's taken up boxing, and comes back with a shiner from time to time.'

I went with him, and he took me into his apartment. His wife and kid were out which was fortunate as she was more garrulous than he. He found a tube of ointment.

'Rub this in every two hours. I bet you won't know you have had a bruise in a couple of days.'

I thanked him, said I had work to do, shook his hand and returned to my apartment. I rubbed in the ointment, then realising it was getting on for 17.00, and I hadn't eaten all day, I opened a can of soup and heated it.

I spent a long, restless night, wondering and worrying. The following morning, I found the bruise was turning yellow, but my head was still sore.

I had a heavy day ahead of me, and I reached the office just after 08.30. Once at my desk, I had no time to think of Klaus, Glenda or Marsh. I had a lunch date with a client and sold him five expensive calculators. After lunch, satisfied with my sale, I drove back to my office block. As I was getting out of the car, Sheriff Thomson materialised.

'Hi, citizen!'

'Hey, Joe!'

He regarded me with his cop eyes.

'You had an accident?'

'Golf ball,' I said shortly. 'I forgot to duck. How's life, Joe?'

'Fair.' He wiped the end of his nose with the back of his hand. 'You seen Mrs Marsh?'

I kept my face expressionless.

'No. I've been nursing this bruise over the weekend.'

'She had a date with me to photograph the jail. She didn't show up.'

'Maybe she forgot.'

'Seems she's pulled out.' Thomson gave me his cop stare, 'I went along to her apartment, right opposite yours, and the janitor tells me she left at seven yesterday morning with luggage.'

'Is that right?' I tried to meet his stare, but failed. I looked down the street for something better to look at. 'That's surprising. Maybe she had an urgent call or something.'

'Yeah. Well, you've got business. I've got business. See you,' and nodding, he walked on.

For a long moment, I stared after him, then hurried up to my office. I had a feeling of fear, but there was nothing I could do except wait for Klaus' move.

I waited for five long, uneasy days. It was when I had finished work and had returned to the loneliness of my apartment that the pressure was on. I found I was pacing the floor, my heart beating sluggishly, my mind darting like a mouse trying to avoid a cat. How I longed for Glenda during these hours.

On the fifth evening, an express delivery arrived as I was unlocking my apartment door. The envelope was bulky, and as I signed for it, I knew the wait was over.

I shut and locked my apartment door. Then going over to my armchair, I sat down and ripped open the envelope. It contained eight coloured photographs, needle sharp, and obviously taken with a powerful telescopic lens.

Shot 1 showed Glenda in her bikini on the beach and I approaching her.

Shot 2 showed Glenda on her back, naked, and I too naked, kneeling over her.

Shot 3 showed me covering her, and Marsh, his face a snarling mask, coming from behind the sand shrubs.

Shots 4, 5, 6 showed Marsh and me fighting like savages.

Shot 7 showed me standing over Marsh, horror on my face, and blood on his.

Shot 8 showed me standing in the trench, digging.

As I looked at the photographs, a Siberian wind seemed to be blowing over me. The deadly trap had been carefully sprung, I had walked into it, and the teeth had snapped shut.

I now realised why Harry had shoved me close to the body to let the hidden photographer get his shot, and why Harry had given me the trenching tool so I dug for a few minutes before Joe took over.

My hopes of outwitting Edwin Klaus and telling him to go to hell abruptly evaporated.

As I was staring at the photographs, I heard a sound that made me stiffen and drop the photographs in an incriminating puddle at my feet: the sad, forlorn tune of a negro spiritual, played on a harmonica. The player was outside my front door.

Getting steadily to my feet, my mind in a dazed panic, I threw open the door. Joe, looking enormous, still wearing the white singlet and black slacks, was propping up the opposite wall. He gave me his wide, dazzling smile and slipped the harmonica into his shirt pocket.

'Evening, Mr Lucas. The boss wants to chat you up. Let's go.'

Leaving the door open, I went back and picked up the photographs, stuffed them into the envelope and locked the envelope in my desk drawer.

It didn't cross my mind to refuse to go with this negro. I was trapped, and I knew it.

We rode down the elevator. Parked outside the apartment block was a dusty, beaten-up Chevvy.

Joe was humming to himself. He unlocked the car door, reached across and flicked up the lock button of the passenger's seat. I went around the car and got in.

He set the car in motion. At this time in the evening the streets were almost deserted. He drove carefully, still humming to himself, then he said suddenly, 'You happy about your car, Mr Lucas? I sure worked on it. Plenty of wax.'

I sat motionless, my clenched fists between my knees. I couldn't bring myself to speak to him.

He glanced at me.

'You know something, Mr Lucas? I was just another nigger before Mr Klaus picked me up. Now, it's all different. I've got a pad of my own. I get regular money. I've got a girl. I've got time to play my harmonica. You go along with Mr Klaus. That's the smart thing to do. He's a real power man.' He chuckled. 'Power means money, Mr Lucas. That's what I like – real money. Not piddly dimes, but fat dollars.'

Still, I said nothing.

He leaned forward and pressed down on a cassette and the car was filled with strident beat music.

We drove for some fifteen minutes, then he turned off the highway and headed into the country. When the cassette finished, he again looked at me.

'Mr Lucas, sir, I know you're in a spot of trouble. Take my tip, Mr Lucas, and go along. Don't dig your own grave. You do what the boss tells you, and you'll be happy.'

'Screw you,' I said, in no mood to take his advice.

He giggled.

'That's it, Mr Lucas. That's what they all say to me, but this nigger boy knows what he's talking about. Just don't dig own grave.'

He swung the car into a narrow road and drove to a ranch-style house, half hidden by trees. He stopped before a farm gate, and a figure emerged from the shadows. It was Harry. He opened the gate, and as Joe drove forward, Harry waved to me. I ignored him. Joe drove to the entrance of the house and pulled up.

Lights showed in six windows.

Joe got out and went around and opened my door.

'Here we are, Mr Lucas.'

As I got out, Benny appeared.

'Come on, fink,' Benny said, and catching hold of my arm in a vice-like grip, he shoved me roughly towards the open front door. He propelled me along a passage and into the big living-room.

The room had a picture window that looked on to the distant lights of Sharnville. There were comfortable lounging chairs, a big settee before an empty fireplace. To the right was a well-stocked bar. There was a TV set and a stereo radio. Three good-looking rugs covered the floor, but the room gave off the atmosphere of being rented, and not lived in.

'Want a drink, fink?' Benny asked as I came to rest in the middle of the room. 'The boss is busy right now. Have a Scotch, huh?'

I went to one of the armchairs and dropped into it.

'Nothing,' I said.

He shrugged and went out, closing the door.

I sat there, my heart thumping, my hands clammy. After a while I heard Joe playing his harmonica: the same sad tune.

I sat there for some ten minutes, then the door opened abruptly and Klaus came in. He shut the door, paused to regard me, then came over to sit in a chair opposite mine. His teak-wood face was expressionless.

'I apologise for keeping you waiting, Mr Lucas. I have many affairs to attend to.' Then as I said nothing, he went on, 'What do you think of the photographs?' He lifted his eyebrows inquiringly. 'I thought they were exceptionally good. They, alone, would convince any judge that you had murdered Marsh, don't you think?'

I looked at him, hating him.

'What do you want?'

'We will come to that in a moment.' He leaned back, resting his small brown hands in his lap. 'Let me first spell out your position, Mr Lucas. You were foolish enough to write to Glenda. I have that letter, arranging a meeting with her. I have the trenching tool with your fingerprints on it. I have the stained trunk mat. I have only to hand the photographs with your letter, the trenching tool and the trunk mat to Sheriff Thomson for you to go away for life.'

'Does Glenda know about this?' I had to know.

'Of course. She does exactly what I tell her to do as you are going to do exactly what I tell you to do. She will be the principal witness at your trial if you are stupid enough not to co-operate with me. She will swear she saw you kill her husband. Make no mistake about this, Mr Lucas, unless you do exactly what I want you to do.'

'And what do you want me to do?' I sat forward, registering what he had said: *She does exactly what I tell her to do.* This must mean that Glenda whom I loved was also a victim of Klaus' blackmail. This knowledge gave me a feeling of relief. She had been forced to betray me!

'First, let me tell you a story,' Klaus said. 'Some forty years ago, your patron, Farrell Brannigan and I were small-time tellers in a small-time bank in the Midwest. We were close friends. We shared the same tiny apartment, and we were both ambitious. Brannigan is a self-righteous man. While he worked nights on banking law and so on, I was out on the town. I got involved with a woman.' He paused to stare thoughtfully at me. 'It is necessary for me to tell you this so you can understand why you are here, and why I am going to tell you what I want you to do.'

I said nothing.

'This woman was expensive,' Klaus went on. 'I was young. To hold her, I had to spend money on her, and I had very little money as a small-time teller. I found what I thought to be a safe way of taking money from the bank. Because of this woman, I embezzled some six thousand dollars. I felt safe to do this as the bank audit wasn't due for six months. I spent five thousand dollars amusing this woman, then a month before the audit, I backed a certain winner, running in the Kentucky Derby, using the last thousand dollars. I won ten thousand dollars. There would be no problem about repaying the six thousand I had stolen, but I had reckoned without Brannigan. Without my knowledge, Brannigan conducted a bank audit on his own. I had no idea why he stayed night after night at the bank, and I didn't care. I thought he was preparing for his next bank examination. He did the audit because he wanted to add to his experience. Brannigan always sought experience. It didn't take him long to find that I had stolen six thousand dollars. Although it is now some forty years ago, I can still see him, very self-righteous, accusing me of embezzlement. We were close friends. I trusted him. I admitted I had stolen the money, but I would repay it. When he learned I had backed a horse – something that was utterly repellent to him – he said I was not only a thief, but a gambler, and I had no right to work in any bank. He gave me no chance to repay the money.' For a brief moment, Klaus' slate-grey eyes lit up in a glare of unnerving fury. Then the light in his eyes vanished. But that one brief glimpse warned me how dangerous he was. 'He was then, and still is, a self-righteous man. He went to the bank directors and betrayed me. I was jailed for five years.'

I was now listening intently. It began to dawn on me, having seen that maniacal glare, that I could be dealing with a psychopath.

'When you serve a five-year sentence in a tough jail, Mr Lucas, you acquire a new slant on life,' he continued, his voice now quiet and controlled. 'I was finished as a bank official. I had to make a new career for myself. I mixed with all kinds of men when in jail. At the age of thirty, I was very ambitious, so when I came out, I attempted a fraud that would have made me a lot of money, but because of my associates, the fraud turned sour, and I went back to jail for fifteen years. Life in jail, Mr Lucas, makes a man bitter. During those years while I was kept like a caged animal, I thought about Farrell Brannigan. Had he not been such a self-righteous man, I could have put the money back, and I could have been some kind of a banker: not in the same class as Brannigan, because he never stopped working and learning to become the top banker which he now is. I didn't have his drive or talent, but I could have made a reasonable living as a branch manager had he given me the chance. When I came out of jail, Brannigan had become President of the Californian National Bank. I had had fifteen years in which to think about my future. I had made several useful contacts with other prisoners. I had gained useful experience. Through my contacts and my experience, I have made a lot of money. I am now about to retire. I plan to live in luxury somewhere in the sun.' He paused, then went on, 'But before I do so, I have a score to settle with Brannigan. I have waited many years for this opportunity, and this will be my last operation before I retire.'

I continued to listen intently, studying this man, watching his movements, listening to the snarl in his voice.

'Well now, Mr Lucas, this is where you come in,' Klaus continued. 'Through the press and other media, Brannigan now boasts he owns the safest bank in the world. That is the boast of a self-righteous man and a challenge I intend to take up. I intend to break into his safest bank in the world, and strip out his vault which has cash and jewellery his clients have entrusted with him: hidden cash to avoid tax and uninsured jewellery. Although Brannigan is a self-righteous man, he is also vain. The one thing that can hit him, as nothing else can is to be made a world laughing-stock. By cleaning out his safest bank in the world, he will be reduced to midget size.' Again the slate-grey eyes blazed. Klaus leaned forward and stared at me, his mouth twitching. He pointed a small brown finger at me. 'You made the bank safe, Mr Lucas, and now, you are going to make it unsafe!'

So there it was: an impossible task, but, at least, I now knew his blackmail conditions.

My voice husky, I said, 'I made it safe, and it remains safe. There is nothing I can do to make it unsafe. I assure you of that. The electronic devices, protecting the vault, are foolproof. It is no idle boast that this bank is the safest bank in the world. If you have to get even with Brannigan, you will have to dream up some other sick idea.'

Klaus looked down at his small hands.

'Fifteen years is a long time for a young, ambitious man like you, Mr Lucas, to rot in jail. I know from experience. I assure you that unless you come up with a foolproof plan to break into that vault, I will send all the evidence I have against you to Sheriff Thomson, and you will not only be ruined in Sharnville, but you will most certainly get a life sentence.' He stood up. 'You have seven days, Mr Lucas. At nine o'clock next Friday night, you will receive a telephone call. You will either say yes or no. If it is yes, then we will meet again. If it is no, the Sheriff will call on you.'

He left the room, and Benny came in.

'Move with the feet, fink,' he said. 'Joe'll cart you home.'

During the drive back, it was impossible to think. The car rocked with strident beat music, going full blast from a cassette. As Joe drove, he kept shouting. 'Yes, man! Yes, man! Dig-dig-dig!'

He pulled up outside my apartment and switched off the cassette. It was at that moment of silence that the full impact of my talk with Klaus hit me.

As I got out of the car, Joe leaned forward and caught hold of my arm.

'Use your head, Mr Lucas,' he said earnestly. 'You go along with the boss, and you'll be in the rich gravy. Don't dig your own grave.'

I pulled free, and walked across the sidewalk, into my apartment block and rode up in the elevator.

As I was unlocking my front door, the door of the opposite apartment jerked open.

'Quick!' Glenda said breathlessly, and pushing by me, she ran into my living-room.

I moved inside, closed the door, then turned and faced her.

In black stretch-pants and a red T-shirt, she stood in the middle of the room. Her full breasts rose and fell with her laboured breathing. Her face was chalk white and her eyes were wild.

As we stared at each other, I heard, through the open window, a car start up and drive away.

4

We sat side by side on the settee, my arm around her, her head against my shoulder. The yielding softness of her body against mine told me, as nothing else could do, how much I loved her. Her hands gripped mine. Her red hair was against my fading bruise.

The roar of the traffic, coming through the open window, the sound of Jebson's TV coming up from below, the whine of the elevator as it moved between floors made a background of noise I scarcely registered.

Her hands tightened their grip.

'I feel so terrible!' she said. 'How was I to know I would find someone like you! Oh, Larry, I am so sorry!' She raised her face and her arm went around my neck. With her lips against mine, her tongue darting, Klaus faded from my mind. My fingers found the top of her stretch pants, hooked in and pulled down. I peeled them off her as she gave a sighing moan.

We rolled off the settee on to the floor. My hands slid under her.

Arching her body, she received me, and my world exploded as she clutched and strained.

After what seemed a long period of time, I became aware of the sound of the church clock chiming ten: heavy, sonorous strokes.

Then she caressed my face and rolled away from me, got up, leaving me lying there, satiated, aware now only of the smell of dust from the carpet, but utterly relaxed.

I heard the water running in the bathroom. Forcing myself to my feet, I pulled on my slacks as she came from the bathroom and walked slowly to the settee.

'A drink, Larry,' she said. 'A big one.'

I made two outsized whiskys, and not bothering with ice, I came over and sat beside her. She drank the neat whisky in two gulps, then let the glass drop on the carpet.

'Larry, darling!' She turned to stare at me, her big eyes glittering. 'I love you! Please believe that!' She held up her hand. 'Don't say anything yet ... just listen to me. I swear to you if I had had any idea what that devil was planning, I wouldn't have done what I did! I swear it to you! Please listen! Let me explain.'

I put my hand on hers.

'You are in the same trap as I am. That's right, isn't it?'

'Oh, yes, but it is a different kind of trap.' She leaned back and closed her eyes. 'Larry, I am nothing. I have never been anything but nothing. I won't tell you about my background. God! It was sleazy. That's the only word. I ran away from my parents. For ten years, I had dozens of jobs, and they all finished up in some sordid bedroom with me fighting off the man who was employing me. A year ago, I got a job at a motel. What a job! There I met Alex. He had money. He ran a Caddy. When he offered marriage, I jumped at it ... anything to get away from fumbling hands and slinging hash. In his crazy, vicious way he was madly in love with me. To me, he was a meal ticket, and nothing more. He had a big business, handling hot cars. I didn't care. I had kicked around long enough not to bother about which side of the law I was on. All I wanted was a shelter.

Alex was crazy about golf. He taught me. We played every day. We had a nice bungalow. When he was working, I just slopped around. We had a coloured woman to clean. Then one day, he came back early, looking as if he had been run over by a truck. He was in a terrible state. His face swollen, his eyes black, caked blood on his coat. He had been worked over. All his guts, and he had lots of guts, had drained out of him. He told me he and I had to work for Klaus. I didn't know what he was talking about, but the sight of him scared me. He said Klaus had visited him in his garage, and had said he wanted Alex and me to do a job for him. Alex told him to go to hell. Then three men walked in and nearly killed Alex. They beat him silly. They took Alex's guts from him like a surgeon takes out an appendix. He was now a fat, slobbering creature who horrified me. I said no one was going to tell me what to do, and I was leaving him. Then Benny and Joe walked in. While Alex sat crying, they gagged me and took the guts out of me with a strap. By the time they had finished, I was as craven as Alex.' She paused to pick up her fallen glass. 'I'll have another drink, Larry.'

Feeling cold and sick, I made her another whisky.

'That's how it was, Larry,' she said, and drank. 'Klaus has told you about his plan to break into the Sharnville bank?'

'He's told me.'

'He's a devil. Make no mistake about that. He found out you and Brannigan played golf together. He sent Joe to put water in Brannigan's gas tank so you and I could meet. His idea was for me to come to Sharnville with his phoney reporting setup. He thought I could persuade you to tell me about the security of the bank.' She ran her fingers through her red hair. 'If only you had, Larry! Alex could be alive now.'

'He should have known,' I said.

She lifted her hands in despair.

'It was a long shot which didn't work. Then he told me he would blackmail you into giving me the information, and he told me what I had to do. With the threat of another beating, I hadn't the guts to refuse. I thought they would just take photographs of us making love, and that would be enough. I swear I had no idea that Alex would be involved, and they would murder him.' She looked directly at me. 'You must hate me for what I have done to you, but if you had been beaten as I have, maybe you would understand.'

'Of course I don't hate you! I could never do that,' I said. 'This is something we have to work out together. You are the one woman who has ever meant anything to me.' I took her hands in mine. 'I have seven days to say either yes or no. This has dropped on me like an avalanche. My mind isn't working properly, but let us look at the situation we are both faced with. Klaus plans to rob the bank, using me to tell him how to do it. He has enough evidence against me to send me to jail for life. That is his ace card, but I also have an ace card. I could go to Brannigan, and tell him the whole story. He is, as Klaus has said, a righteous man, but he wouldn't stand for blackmail. I'm sure of that. He knows Klaus is a liar and a thief. He could use his power to nail Klaus, and get me off this hook. I would be finished in Sharnville, but at least, I wouldn't go to jail. We two could go somewhere, and I could begin again. As I see it right now, I must talk to Brannigan.'

Glenda closed her eyes and shivered.

'Have you forgotten you are dealing with a devil, Larry? A devil who didn't hesitate to kill Alex so he could blackmail you? We two won't go away together. How I wish it was as easy as that.' She paused, then went on, 'If you don't do what he wants, he is going to have me murdered as he had Alex murdered.'

I stared at her, not believing what I had heard.

'Murdered? What do you mean?'

'Klaus has already anticipated that you would go to Brannigan. Why do you think I am here, Larry? Why do you think he has allowed me to see you again? He told me to spell out the message. He will have me murdered so it will look as if you killed me as he made it look as if you killed Alex.'

Again, I felt as if a Siberian wind was blowing over me. I was once again a mouse darting here and there to avoid the cat's claws.

'If we are going to escape from this trap, Larry,' Glenda went on, 'you must tell Klaus how to break into the bank, but this is up to you.' She got up and began to move around the room. 'He is a devil! I'm so frightened! I don't want to die, Larry. I want to share my life with you. I don't give a damn if we have no money … just so long as we are together. Do you really care if this bank is robbed? Every day banks are being robbed, and who cares? You have only to tell him how to do it, and we are free!'

I hesitated, staring at her.

'But, Glenda, I made it safe! You must understand! If Klaus breaks into that bank, everything I have worked for, my position in Sharnville, the years and years of grinding study goes into a puddle of mud.'

She put her hands to her eyes.

'All right, Larry. Yes, I understand, then my life takes second place.'

As if on cue, the front door burst open, and Benny and Joe came in. Joe caught hold of Glenda and jerked her to the open door. Benny moved up to me and gave me a shove with his open hand, sending me reeling.

'Okay, fink,' he said. 'You now know the photo. The next time you see this babe, she'll be a bloody mess unless you do what you're told,' and they left, hustling Glenda between them, and the door slammed behind them.

Unsteadily, I went to the window and watched them push Glenda into the Chevvy, then watched them drive away.

I sat down. It was still a nightmare, and I longed for the moment when I woke up to find this hadn't happened: that this was only a terrifying dream.

The church clock struck eleven. Jebson's TV set suddenly snapped off. There was silence, except for the distant roar of the traffic and sitting still, I had to face the fact that this was no nightmare.

I heard Glenda's voice, shaking with panic: *Do you really care if the bank is robbed?*

I thought of Farrell Brannigan, and what he had done for me. I remembered what Dixon had said. Brannigan had no mercy for anyone who stepped out of turn. He was a righteous man. He would have no mercy for me if I went to him and told him this blackmail story. My immediate reaction had been to go to him, but now, thinking about it, I realised he would treat me as he had treated Klaus forty years ago.

It was hard for me to believe that Klaus would have Glenda murdered, but, I told myself, he had ruthlessly arranged her husband's murder. His threat could become a reality, and this was unthinkable.

You have only to tell me how to do it, and we're free!

I could submit to Klaus' blackmail and tell him how to break into the bank. I considered this. Only Brannigan. Alec Manson and I knew of the soft underbelly of the bank's security. If Klaus succeeded in robbing the bank, Brannigan would be immediately discounted. The searchlight would then concentrate on Manson and myself. Brannigan would never have chosen Manson to manage the safest bank in the world unless he was sure Manson was above reproach. The police would probe into Manson's background. They would find, as I knew, he lived simply, and he was a dedicated banker, so the searchlight would concentrate on me. I was the one who had made the bank safe. I knew far better than Manson how the electronic gimmicks worked. These gimmicks were so safe, no thief could get into the bank without inside information. This information was held by Brannigan, Manson and myself. When they had discounted Brannigan and Manson, they would select me as suspect No. 1.

I was being threatened by Klaus with a life sentence for murdering Marsh. According to Glenda, he would have her murdered, and make it seem I was her killer if I didn't cooperate with him. Yet if I did, and I broke down under police interrogation, I could still face a long jail sentence.

There must be a way out of this trap!

I had seven days.

In seven days, I had to come up with a solution to save myself!

Another Monday!

My desk was piled with work. The telephone bell constantly rang. Bill Dixon, calling from 'Frisco, came through with the final details of our new building.

'This is going to be a big one, Larry,' he said excitedly. 'They have approved the extra extension. We have really got off the pad.'

I listened, made notes, assured him I could handle my end of it and hung up. The pressure was such I couldn't even think of Klaus, but he was at the back of my mind, pushed into my subconscious, but ready to appear the moment I could pause to think.

Mary Oldham, my secretary, a plump, middle-aged woman who was efficiency itself, looked around my door.

'Sheriff Thomson, Mr Lucas, asking for you.'

I stiffened, my heart skipping a beat as Thomson stalked into my office.

'Hi, citizen,' he said, 'Police business. You're busy, I'm busy, but police business is more than busy.'

'Okay, Joe, make it fast. What is it?'

The telephone bell rang, and I picked up the receiver. It was the builder's contractor. We talked costs for a couple of minutes, then I told him to talk to Bill Dixon, and hung up.

'What is it, Joe?' I asked impatiently.

'Glenda Marsh,' Thomson said. 'She's quit town. She's a phoney.'

'What does that mean, and what has that to do with me?' I forced myself to meet his probing eyes.

'This woman came here to do a reportage for *The Investor* ... right?'

'So she told me,' I said.

'Yeah. So she told you. She poked around, took photographs, had a date with me to photograph the jail, then didn't show, and has left town.' He took out a crumpled pack of cigarettes from his shirt pocket and lit up. '*The Investor* is an important paper. So I asked myself why this woman should suddenly quit town. I contacted *The Investor*, and they tell me they don't know her and they don't employ freelance photographers. What do you make of that?'

I had to play this cool, and with an effort, I shrugged, waving my hand impatiently.

'Look, Joe, I'm up to my eyes in work. For all I know, and frankly, I don't give a damn, she was an opportunist. Lots of freelance journalists do the same thing – claiming they work for an important magazine to get interviews. Then they write up articles and try to sell them. It happens all the time.'

Thomson leaned forward to tap off his ash into my ash bowl.

'Yeah, could be.' He sucked at his cigarette, then went on, 'I am Sheriff of Sharnville. It is my job to protect this town. Sharnville has the safest bank in the world, and lots of wealthy citizens. It's my job to watch over them, and the bank. That's what I get paid for. When a woman like Marsh arrives on the scene, takes photographs, chats up our more wealthy citizens who, thinking she is representing *The Investor*, talk their fat heads off, because getting coverage in a magazine of that standing is a status symbol, and then I find out she is a phoney, I start looking for trouble. I've talked to a number of our wealthy citizens, and learn they have been boasting to this woman about the money they stash away in the Californian National Bank.' He made a grimace. 'When you get a guy making big money, get him to drink a few martinis, let a pretty woman soft-talk him, he runs at the mouth.' His little cop eyes were like granite. 'When she talked to you, did she ask you anything about the security of our bank?'

Keeping my face expressionless, I said, 'No, but she did ask me to give her an introduction to Manson, which I did.'

'I know that. I've talked to Manson.' He kept staring at me. 'So she didn't ask you about the security of the bank?

You know more about the security setup than Manson does, don't you?'

'You can say that.' Then the telephone bell rang. This gave me time to get my second wind. It was Bill Dixon asking about a computer I had ordered. I spent longer than necessary telling him the exact measurements and where the electric feed should be.

Thomson continued to sit, staring at me, but by the time I had finished talking to Bill I had steadied down.

'Look, Joe, you can see I'm working under pressure,' I said. 'Mrs Marsh didn't ask about the security of the bank. Is that all you want to know?'

'Just how safe is the security of the bank?' He showed no sign of going.

'As safe as could be.'

'Now, suppose a smart bunch of thieves decided to break into the bank. Do you think they could do it?'

This was now moving onto very thin ice. I must not commit myself. Klaus could force me to tell him how to make a break-in.

'I would have thought their chances would be a hundred to one against,' I said.

'Is that right?' Thomson dropped more ash into my ash bowl. 'Manson says they wouldn't stand a ghost of a chance. He says the security of the bank is more than a hundred per cent.'

'You're making this difficult for me, Joe,' I said. 'Just how much did Manson tell you about the electronic safety controls I have installed in the bank?'

'Not a thing. He said he was satisfied no one could break in, and that's all he told me.'

'He is right to a point, but there is always some freak chance we haven't thought of.'

'Listen to me, citizen. I was elected sheriff of Sharnville three years ago. The crime rate of this town, because I am always looking ahead, run out undesirables, and have a smart lot of men, is the lowest in the state, and I intend to keep it that way. This Marsh woman bothers me. She could be a front for a gang with eyes on our bank. I don't say she is, but she could be, and it is my business to check on people like her. She tried pretty hard to get information from Manson about the security of the bank, but failed, but that doesn't mean the gang – if there is a gang – will give up. Just suppose there is an attack on the bank, I wouldn't get elected sheriff for my next term, and that would hit me where I live. Understand?'

'I think you can relax, Joe,' I said. 'I understand your position and your responsibility, but the bank is as safe as it can be.'

'That's what Manson said, but you said a hundred to one against. What's the one?'

'I don't know, but there is always some bright boy who could dream up a bright idea,' I said. 'The unexpected has always to be taken into consideration.'

He stubbed out his cigarette and lit another.

'That's right. Now, Manson and you are the only two in this town who know how the security works ... right?'

My secretary looked in.

'Mr Harriman is waiting, Mr Lucas.'

'Just a few minutes,' I said, then looking at Thomson, I went on, 'Mr Brannigan also knows.'

'Suppose a smart gang kidnapped you or Manson or both of you and put you under pressure? It happens. Could they bust into the bank once he or you talked.'

'No.'

He stared thoughtfully at me.

'Even if they really give you the works?'

'We might be forced to tell them how the gimmicks worked, but they still wouldn't have the expertise to make them work.'

'And yet you said some bright boy might dream up a bright idea. What did you mean by that?'

I became aware that a trickle of sweat was running down my face.

'There is always a remote chance that someone with top-class electronic expertise just might be able to unscramble my gimmicks, but it is very, very unlikely.'

He thought for a moment, then nodding, he got to his feet.

'Thanks for your time. I'm now waiting to hear from Washington. If she has a record, I'll trouble you again. No smart gang is going to bust into our bank while I am sheriff. I'll get clearance from Mr Brannigan for Manson and you to explain to me just how secure this bank is so I can protect it.' He tapped his long, hawk-like nose. 'I can smell trouble a mile off, and I'm smelling it now,' then with a curt nod, he left me.

It took me three evenings of hard thinking to make up my mind how to deal with Klaus. The threat to Glenda and the threat of a life sentence for me were far too deadly for me to attempt a rash bluff, but that didn't mean I intended to surrender to Klaus' pressure. I knew once Klaus' people broke into the bank, I would be suspect No. 1. The police heat would be intense. I would be finished in Sharnville, even if I wasn't arrested, so I had to plan ahead. If I could find no way out of this blackmail situation, and I was finally forced to do what Klaus demanded, I had to think of a new future, not only for myself, but also for Glenda. Although I was kept busy during the day, my nights were now spent in setting up a two-prong plan: either, somehow, to outwit this ruthless embezzler, or if he outwitted me, at least, to secure a trouble-free future with Glenda, far away from Sharnville.

On the morning of the seventh day, as I was getting out of my car, Sheriff Thomson wandered up.

'Hi, citizen!'

'Hello, Joe.'

He wiped the end of his nose with the back of his hand, then said, 'Glenda Marsh has no record. Maybe you've got something: she could be an opportunist, using *The Investor* to get interviews, then lost her nerve and pulled out.'

'Fine,' I said, keeping my face expressionless.

'Yeah, but all the same I'll keep an eye on the bank.'

'Mr Brannigan will appreciate that.'

'You might tell him when next you play golf with him.' He stared at me, then went on, 'This idea of mine about you or Manson getting kidnapped is a thought. Now, listen to me: if ever you get a feeling you're being watched or followed, alert me. I'll put a guard on you. I've said the same to Manson.'

'Thanks.' Then giving him back his own dialogue, I said, 'Well, you're busy. I'm busy. See you,' and I went up to my office.

For the moment, I thought, I had Thomson off my back, but I knew once Klaus broke into the bank, Thomson would be after my hide.

On this seventh day, somehow I got through my business chores. Around 19.00, I had a steak dinner at the Howard Johnson, then returned to my apartment. I sat and waited.

At 21.00, the telephone bell rang. I lifted the receiver. Over the line came the sound of the negro spiritual, played on a harmonica.

'The answer is yes,' I said.

'Okay, man,' Joe said. 'See you outside in five minutes.'

The dusty Chevvy was waiting as I left my apartment block. Joe leaned over and opened the passenger door and I slid in.

'Man! You're sure doing the right thing,' he said. 'I was scared you would try and act smart. You know something, Mr Lucas? I'm just a nigger boy, but I dig Miss Glenda. I would sure hate for Benny to take her apart, and that's what would have happened if you had tried something smart.'

I hesitated for a moment, then knowing I would have to work with this man, I decided to go along with him.

'I have no choice, Joe,' I said. 'I have to do what I'm told.'

'You sure do, Mr Lucas, but don't worry your brains. You'll get on the gravy train same as me.'

'That's what you say. Maybe Klaus isn't as smart as he thinks he is.'

Again Joe laughed.

'He is, Mr Lucas. I wouldn't be sticking my neck out if I wasn't sure of that. I've worked for him now for two years. He's never put a foot wrong. Before I worked for him, I was in and out of jail all the time, and, brother, do I hate jail. Yes ... Mr Klaus is smart all right ... real smart.'

'There's always a time to put your foot wrong,' I said. 'Robbing the Californian National Bank could be his first time.'

'Not with you to tell us how to do it, Mr Lucas. The boss explained. If anything goes wrong, you and Miss Glenda don't exist any more. It's up to you to fix it.' He laughed. 'And I'm sure you wouldn't want Benny to knock off Miss Glenda nor you.'

'I can tell Klaus how to get into the bank,' I said, 'but it could still go wrong, Joe. You could go away for twenty years.'

Joe glanced at me, no longer smiling.

'Just stop flapping with your mouth. I go away for twenty years, you and Miss Glenda go into a hole six feet deep.' He leaned forward and pressed down the cassette. The car was filled with strident jazz, and that was the end of the conversation.

We arrived at the ranch house. Harry was there to open the gate. Benny was waiting and took me into the big living-room.

'Want a drink, fink?' he asked. 'The boss is busy.'

'Nothing.' I sat down.

I waited some ten minutes, then Klaus came in. He went over to the desk and sat behind it.

'My congratulations, Mr Lucas. You wouldn't be here unless you had decided to co-operate. This is good news. It tells me you are as smart as I thought you were.'

'I hope you are as smart as your black boy thinks you are,' I said. 'You have opposition. Your non-smart move was to send Glenda here as a reporter. Her cover has been blown. After she talked to Manson about the security of the bank, Thomson has been alerted that there could be a raid on the bank. The red light has gone up. Thomson is dangerous ...' I went on to tell him of Thomson's suspicions of Glenda, how he had contacted the FBI, how he had found she had no record, and of his idea that either Manson or I, or both, could be kidnapped to get information of the bank security.

Klaus sat still, his small hands resting on his desk, his slate-grey eyes like blobs of ice, regarding me.

'Never mind about the sheriff,' he said. 'I have already anticipated trouble from him, and I will take care of him.

Your job, Mr Lucas, is to tell me how to get into the bank's vault.'

'Let us suppose you do get into the vault,' I said. 'Both Manson and I would become suspects. Manson, on his record, would be ruled out, but Thomson, knowing I had associated with Glenda, would consider me suspect No. 1. So before co-operating with you, I want to know what is in it for me?'

His thin lips moved into a smile.

'I was expecting you to say that, Mr Lucas. You will, of course, be suspect No. 1. You will have to leave Sharnville immediately after the break-in. I have told you, I am a rich man. I am not interested in the money my people will take from the bank. All I want is to cut Brannigan down to size. The vault will produce at least three million dollars. I have told my people that your pay-off is to be a million, so you and Glenda can go away somewhere and enjoy the proceeds. I would suggest South America. You would both be safe there. With a million dollars you could live very comfortably.'

I believed him as I believed there was a Santa Claus.

'On those conditions,' I said, 'I will tell you about the bank security.'

Again the blobs of ice regarded me.

'That's what I want to know.'

'Have you been to the bank?'

He shook his head.

'The soft underbelly of any bank is a gang rushing in and taking hostages,' I said. 'This can't happen to this bank. All cash in and out transactions are computer controlled. A client enters the lobby, signs his cheque with a computer pen, drops his cheque into a slot and out comes the money. If he pays in money, he writes on a special form, drops in the money and out comes a receipt. The bank's staff are seen only on close-circuit TV screens. There is no way for a gang to get at the staff. They are up on the second floor where the cash is, and there is no way for any unauthorised person to get up there. Recognised clients are given a small electric gimmick that allows them up to the second floor. If this gimmick is lost or stolen, the TV screen alerts the guardian it isn't the client and the elevator wouldn't work.'

Klaus raised his hand.

'I'm not interested in taking hostages, Mr Lucas. I want my people to get into the vault and strip it out. Now tell me how this can be done.'

'The bank closes on Friday evening at 16.00. The staff leave around 17.50. The bank opens on Monday morning at 09.00,' I said. 'Because of the electronic security there is only one patrolling guard. He works in shifts with three other guards. He patrols outside the bank. He has a heated sentry box at the bank's entrance, but every hour, he walks around the outside of the bank. The entrance to the bank is guarded by steel doors which are controlled by a photoelectric cell. There is no problem in getting into the lobby of the bank. I have a gimmick that will open the doors. It is a matter of careful timing. When the guard is at the back of the bank on his patrol, your people move in. Once in, they are faced with the vault's door. Now this door is made of fire-resisting steel. No one, if they worked for a solid week, with special equipment, could even dent it.'

Klaus made an impatient movement.

'Never mind the details.' There was a snap in his voice. 'How do I get my people in?'

'The vault door is operated by a voice print,' I told him.

His eyes narrowed.

'What does that mean?'

'At exactly 08.30 every morning, except Saturdays and Sundays, someone at the Los Angeles head office dials a series of numbers on a special telephone directly wired to the Sharnville bank. By doing this a computer is activated and releases three of the vault's locks. At exactly 08.35, Manson, in his office speaks into a microphone another series of numbers, and his voice activates another computer which releases three other locks and the vault door slides open.'

Klaus stared at me, his face blank as he thought.

'Could anyone, knowing the numbers, speak into Manson's microphone and release the locks?'

'That's what I meant when I said a voice print. It has to be Manson's voice or the computer won't work.'

'You have been ingenious, Mr Lucas.' There was an edge to his voice.

'This is the safest bank in the world.'

He thought for a moment, then said, 'What happens when Manson is on vacation or if he drops dead?'

'That has been taken care of; there is a tape recording of his voice which the computer will accept. Should he be away or something happens to him, someone is authorised to use this recording. All this someone has to do is to drop the cassette into a hidden slot and the vault door opens.'

'And who is this someone?'

I looked steadily at him.

'As I invented this system, it was decided that I should do it.'

He leaned forward.

'You have the cassette?'

'It is in the bank. In the event of an emergency, I go to the bank, produce the cassette and release the three locks. Manson's successor will make another cassette. I will fix the computer to accept his voice and we are back on square A.'

'It would seem, Mr Lucas, the bank trusts you.'

'There are six locks on the vault. I can only open three of them. You are forgetting the other three locks are opened by telephone from head office.' I took out a pack of cigarettes. 'They are not all that trusting.'

'What happens if you drop dead or go to jail for life, Mr Lucas?'

'Brannigan knows where the cassette is.'

He stared down at his hands while he thought. I lit a cigarette and waited.

'The LA end seems to me to be difficult,' he said.

'To you, yes, but not to me. I can handle that. I can get your people into the vault, but getting away with the loot is next to impossible.'

He shrugged.

'That is your problem, Mr Lucas. In return for a million dollars, and for all the incriminating evidence I have against you which I will give you, I would have thought, with your expertise, you would find a solution.'

'So, under duress, you are leaving the entire operation to me?'

'That is the situation. I will finance the operation, and supply men to carry out the operation, but you will be responsible for the plan.'

This was my moment to bluff. I had spent the past five nights thinking how I could outwit this man, and I had arrived at a possible solution.

'I accept on certain conditions.'

The mad light flashed up in his slate-grey eyes.

'You are not in a position to make conditions!'

'There you make a mistake. Because Brannigan exposed you as a small-time embezzler, you want revenge. By stripping out the vault of his 'safest bank in the world', you

79

know you will hit him where he lives. To do this, you haven't hesitated to have Marsh murdered so you can force me to get your people into the vault. That you can kill a man tells me that you have set your mind on cutting Brannigan down to size. The weakness of this plan of yours is that you could have underestimated me, and I could elect to stand trial for a murder I didn't commit. You have a criminal record, and you are known to the police. If you hadn't a record, I wouldn't be in the strong position that I am. If I elect to stand trial, I would talk. I would tell Brannigan and the police the story. The fact that I saved his safest bank in the world, and also his reputation, would put Brannigan very much on my side. With his enormous influence, I could just be found not guilty, but make no mistake about it, Brannigan would come after you, and so would the police. You could go back to jail.' I paused, then went on, 'So don't say I am not in a position to make conditions.'

We stared at each other for a long moment. Klaus then nodded, his mouth twitching.

'You have a point, Mr Lucas. I see I have underestimated you. What are your conditions?'

Keeping my face expressionless, but with a surge of triumph running through me as I realised my bluff was working, I leaned forward and stubbed out my cigarette.

'You talk glibly of paying me a million dollars. Do you imagine I am that much of a sucker to take your word? Do you imagine I don't realise that once I have got your people into the vault and have shown them how to get the loot away, you won't have me murdered as you had Marsh murdered?'

Klaus studied me, then his bleak face relaxed into a false smile.

'How very suspicious you are, Mr Lucas. So what do you propose?'

'I can get your people into the vault, and with a little thinking, I can tell them how to get the loot out,' I said, 'but first you will give me bearer bonds for two hundred and fifty thousand dollars. A million dollars is a nice sum, but I am sure, after the operation, I wouldn't get it, so I am prepared to settle for a quarter. If you are not prepared to give me these bonds, then we both call each other's bluff. I'll have to face trial for a murder I didn't commit, and you won't get your revenge, but you will get Brannigan and the police after you. In six days' time, I will come to you with a complete plan: how to get into the vault and get away with the loot. It'll then be up to you. You either have the bonds for me or I don't handle the operation.'

'And how do I know, Mr Lucas, that once I give you the bonds, you won't disappear?'

'I'm not likely to do that while you hold Glenda hostage.' I got to my feet. 'Think it over. On Thursday night at nine o'clock, I will be waiting for Joe to bring me to you. I'll have my side of the deal set up. You have yours.'

Feeling much more in control of this nightmare situation, I walked out of the room, and into the lobby.

Benny was leaning against the wall, picking his teeth. He straightened when he saw me. I walked by him, opened the front door and walked into the hot night.

Joe was sitting in the Chevvy, playing his harmonica. I got in the car.

'Let's go, Joe,' I said, 'and don't spare the horses.'

He giggled and set the car in motion.

5

As I walked into the outer office on Monday morning, my secretary, Mary Oldham, at her desk, looked up.

'Good morning, Mr Lucas.'

'Hi, Mary! What's the mail like?'

'Lots of it. It's on your desk.' A pause, then she said, 'That's a terrible thing about Sheriff Thomson, isn't it?' I stopped as if I had walked into a brick wall.

'Thomson?' I turned and stared at her. 'What happened?'

'It was on the radio, Mr Lucas. Didn't you catch it?'

'What happened?' I was aware my voice was shrill.

'Late last night: a hit-and-run driver. The poor man was walking to his car when this car deliberately hit him. Three people say they saw the car mount the sidewalk. Sheriff Thomson hadn't a chance.'

The Siberian wind blew over me.

'Is he – is he dead?'

'He's very bad. He's in hospital. They say he is in a serious condition.'

I heard Klaus' dry voice saying: *Never mind about the Sheriff. I have already anticipated trouble from him, and I will take care of him.*

So he had taken care of him. I stood there, feeling the blood leaving my face, then pulling myself together, I mumbled I was sorry and walked into my office. I sat down

82

at my desk. I hadn't time even to think before Bill Dixon breezed in.

'I'm off to 'Frisco, Larry,' he said, and put a pile of papers on my desk. 'More work for you. Lowson wants us to equip them with their office furniture. It's the usual rush job. The details are all here.' He looked at me. 'Did Brannigan give us credit?'

'I didn't get around to seeing him again,' I said, 'but he will. Don't worry about that.'

He grinned.

'That's your worry.' He looked at his watch. 'I must get off. Tough about Thomson. I liked the guy. He was a dedicated cop.'

I turned ice cold.

'Have you more news? I heard he was knocked down.'

'Heard it on the radio as I drove in,' Bill said. 'He died half an hour ago. What kills me is that three jerks actually saw this driver run him down, and none of them got his licence number nor even a description of the car. Some goddamn drunk. Thomson really had crime under control here. Maclain, his deputy, is less than useless. Well, I'm off. See you, Larry,' and he left.

I sat still, staring into space.

I'll take care of him.

First Marsh, now Thomson. Two men dead to achieve a vicious revenge. I remembered what Glenda had said: *He is a devil.* I also remembered that both she and I were equally in the shadow of a violent end.

Then the telephone bell rang, and from then on, I was caught up for the rest of the day in non-stop work.

At 18.00, our small factory at the back of the office block closed for the day. Having cleared my desk, I went down and walked into the big room that housed our setup for repairs, for experiments and for new machines. My three engineers were on the point of leaving. Frank Dodge, my chief engineer, looked enquiringly at me.

'Something special, Mr Lucas?' he asked. 'I'm in no hurry. Something I can do?'

'It's okay, Frank. I just want to work out an idea. You get off.'

When they had gone, I sat down at the bench. I worked until midnight on a gimmick that would unscramble the direct telephone line from the Los Angeles bank to the Sharnville bank. When I had finished, I knew all I had to do was to connect this gimmick with the telephone in Manson's office, and I could open the three locks of the vault.

Taking the gimmick with me, I returned to my apartment. By now I had got over the shock of Thomson's death. He had been dangerous, and I had the feeling he had been hostile to me. Deputy Sheriff Fred Maclain would take his place until the next election. I didn't have to worry about him. He was a big, grossly fat drunk who was good for nothing except bawling out traffic offenders. He could no more cope with a bank break-in than a six-year-old child.

But the red light was up. I knew now that Klaus was utterly ruthless, and nothing would stop him cutting Brannigan down to size. I was sure he would have me murdered if I failed to get his men into the vault. I also felt sure he now wouldn't go ahead with his blackmail threat. I had alerted him that if I was arrested for Marsh's murder, I would talk, and he was more than aware of Brannigan's power. Having discarded this blackmail threat to make me cooperate, he would have to switch threats, and kill Glenda and me if I didn't get his men into the vault.

The next two days passed quickly. I had so much to do in the office, I hadn't time to think of Klaus, but, at night when

I was alone, I thought and planned, and by the third morning, I had a watertight plan for not only getting Klaus' men into the vault, but for them to get away with the loot. I also made other plans to take care of Glenda and myself.

During these three days, there was a tremendous uproar in the local press about Sheriff Thomson's death. The editor said it was shameful, and what were the police doing about it? Even the Mayor joined in. The paper carried a photo of Deputy Sheriff Maclain's fat, bloated face. He declared the police of Sharnville would never rest until they found this drunk driver. No one killed a fine man like Sheriff Thomson and got away with it ... just words that meant nothing.

Thomson's funeral was attended by more than two thousand people. Every leading citizen, including Dixon and myself, were there. It was an experience I will never forget. There was a long queue of important people to shake Mrs Thomson's hand and mutter condolences. I couldn't face that. I told Dixon to represent me, and I moved out of the queue. He gave me an odd look, began to say I should do it, but I walked away.

That night, at 21.00, there was a ring on my doorbell. I had been waiting. I picked up my briefcase, opened the door and found Joe, waiting by the elevator. We rode down together, and got in the Chevvy. I put my briefcase between us.

'So we're going into action, Mr Lucas?' he said, as he started the engine. 'You've got it all fixed?'

'I wouldn't be here if I hadn't,' I said.

'Yeah, man. Soon we'll all be on the gravy train. Man! Does this mean something to me! I've got a girl waiting. Me and she'll take off. I've got it all figured out. We're going to be in the gravy for the rest of our days!'

'Did Benny kill the Sheriff?'

He nodded.

'He sure did. Now, I don't dig Benny, and he sure does a job. That sonofabitch Sheriff was like a boil on my arse. You know something, Mr Lucas? I was driving along, nice and quiet, when this sonofabitch flagged me down. He wanted to know what I was doing in Sharnville. I smelt he hated black people. I told him I was just passing through, and he said for me to keep passing.' Joe giggled. 'He was too smart. When a creep gets too smart, Mr Klaus fixes him, and that sonofabitch was sure fixed.' There was a pause, then he went on, 'You've really got this operation fixed, Mr Lucas?'

'Yes, but it could still go wrong. You could still get twenty years, but that's your funeral.'

'Yeah, man.' He gave a short barking laugh. 'But it sure would be your funeral too.' He drove the car out of the town traffic and onto the highway. 'The boss says there will be three million bucks in the vault. I can't sleep thinking of all that bread.'

This gave me the chance I was waiting for.

'What makes you think you're going to get any bread at all, Joe?' I asked.

I could see his black face in the light from the dashboard. The muscles under his skin tightened.

'What was that again, Mr Lucas?'

'I was just thinking aloud ... forget it.'

'What was that about me not getting my share?' There was a sudden snarl in his voice.

'Forget it. If you're lucky, you'll get it ... if you're lucky.'

He drove in silence for some moments. I lit a cigarette. I hadn't spent the past nights, thinking and planning, for nothing.

Finally, he said anxiously, 'What you mean – lucky?'

'Are you lucky, Joe?'

He thought about this, his face worried.

'Lucky? I guess not. I've never been lucky. I've spent most of my life in jail. I get all the dirty work to do for the boss. No, I guess I ain't lucky.'

'Three million dollars!' I released a low whistle. 'That's a heap of money. I don't know what they have promised you, Joe. Maybe half a million. That's a lot of money for a black boy, but you could be lucky.'

He slowed the car and pulled into a lay-by. He turned and glared at me.

'What are you getting at?' he demanded, alarm in his voice.

'Just stating a fact, Joe. That's a lot of money. What's to stop Benny putting a bullet through your head once he has the loot?'

He stared at me: the whites of his eyes enormous: his thick lips twitching.

'Harry wouldn't let him! What are you getting at?'

'Just warning you, Joe. I'll tell you something. I'm worried about Benny. He's a killer. I've got this operation fixed, but I am getting paid in advance. I'm covered, but you aren't. Now, think, Joe: can you imagine a killer like Benny would let a black boy walk away with five hundred thousand dollars? Ask yourself.'

Sweat broke out on his face.

'Harry will look after me.' He banged his big fists down on the steering wheel. 'I trust Harry.'

'That's fine, but it's news to me. I didn't know any black man could trust any white man when there's big money around. If you can trust Harry to take care of you, then you've nothing to worry about. I was only thinking aloud. Come on, let's get moving.'

He wiped his sweating face with the back of his hand.

'Are you trying to con me, Mr Lucas?'

'It's a lot of money. Think about it. If you can really trust Harry, you have no problem ... a little luck perhaps. Let's go ... your boss is waiting.'

'If Benny tries anything with me,' he muttered, 'I'll fix him.'

I had sown a seed of doubt in his mind, and that's what I wanted to do.

'Sure, but watch him, Joe. When you three get the loot, don't turn your back on him. Now, let's go.'

He sat for a long moment, muttering to himself, then he started the car and drove back onto the highway. I didn't want further talk, so I pressed down the cassette, and the car rocked with beat music.

Harry was at the gate. He waved to me as Joe drove by. I lifted my hand. I would now have to work on Harry. He was a very different proposition to Joe, but I had worked that out too.

As I got out of the car, Benny met me at the front door.

'Hi, fink,' he said. 'The boss is waiting.'

I looked him over, knowing he was the danger. There was a leering expression on his brutal face. I knew I could do nothing with him. I walked by him and into the living-room.

Klaus was sitting at his desk, his small brown hands resting on the blotter.

'Come in, Mr Lucas, and sit down.'

As I sat down, Harry came in and moved over to a distant chair.

I twisted around and looked at him. I wondered about him. He was an unknown factor. He looked tough and cocky as he scratched his beard, but he hadn't Benny's brutal viciousness.

'This is Harry Brett,' Klaus said. 'From now in, Mr Lucas, you and he will work together. You will tell him what you want, and he will arrange it.' He leaned back in his chair. 'I take it you can tell me how to break into the vault and how to get the money out?'

I stared at him.

'Did you have to murder Sheriff Thomson?'

His hands turned into fists and his slate-grey eyes lit up with that maniacal glare.

'Let that be an example to you,' he snarled. 'When anyone obstructs or is likely to obstruct me, I get rid of him. Remember that! Now answer my question: can you tell me how to break into the vault and get the money out?'

'I can, but on my terms.'

'We have gone into that already.' There was a snap in his voice. 'That we will discuss later.'

I glanced at Harry who was listening intently.

'You are forcing me to betray a trust,' I said. 'You are blackmailing me for a murder I didn't commit. The evidence you have against me could put me in jail for years, and you know it is faked evidence. I have a trump card. I could tell Brannigan, and he would come after you, and make no mistake about it, he would nail you. Unless you meet my terms, I am prepared to stand trial, and I know you will also land up in jail. I want advance payment if I tell you how to break into the vault.'

'We have gone into this before,' Klaus said impatiently. 'I will pay you as arranged if you can convince me we can break into the vault and get the money away.'

'We?' I shook my head. 'I don't imagine you will participate. You will be sitting here in safety while your people take the risks.'

Klaus glared at me.

'What risks?'

'The unexpected. If the unexpected happens, your people will go away for twenty years.'

I saw Harry shift uneasily.

Leaning forward, his face a snarling mask, Klaus said, 'And you and your woman will be dead as Marsh and Thomson are dead!'

Looking at him, I now was sure he was mentally unbalanced: he was a psychopath, and I felt a chill crawl up my spine.

'Then let us hope the unexpected doesn't happen,' I said, trying to keep my voice steady. I reached down and picked up my briefcase I had brought with me.

Moving with the quickness of a lizard, Harry was by my side. He snatched the briefcase from me, put it on his desk, flicked up the catches and opened it. A brief glance at its contents satisfied him. He nodded to Klaus, then returned to his chair.

I guessed he might have thought I had brought a gun with me or it might have been a show of efficiency to impress Klaus. Whatever it was, by his lightning movement, I was warned that this man must not be underestimated.

From the briefcase, I took the gimmick I had made and two photoelectric neutralisers and the blueprint of the bank.

I spread the blueprint on the desk.

'Here is the entrance to the bank. Double doors are operated by a photoelectric cell. It is a unique cell with a neutraliser only held by Manson, the head teller and myself. There is no security risk. If someone got hold of the neutraliser, he would only be able to enter the lobby of the bank. He couldn't get into the vault nor get up to the second floor where the staff is. This neutraliser will get your men into the lobby. Getting in has to be timed right when the guard is patrolling. The doors slide back, your men rush in and the doors will automatically close. It shouldn't take them more than thirty seconds. They will have to bring with them a small oxyacetylene cutter to get into the deposit boxes. There will be no problem burning out the locks. It'll take time, but a cutter will do it. The problem, of course, is getting into the vault.' I pointed to the blueprint. 'Here is Manson's office. There are three scanners covering the lobby. Each is activated to take photographs if a beam is broken. Here is the beam,' and I drew a pencil line across the lobby. 'By crawling on hands and knees, your men can reach the elevator without activating the scanner. Using this second neutraliser, they can operate the elevator and get into Manson's office on the second floor.' I picked up the gimmick I had made. 'On Manson's desk is a red telephone. The lead wires must be cut and stripped, then joined with these two wires here,' and I showed him the two loose wires on the gimmick. 'Then using the dial on the red telephone, four numbers must be dialled. The numbers are 2-4-6-8. These numbers will release three of the vault's locks. Then using the cassette of Manson's voice, the other three locks will be released and the vault door opens. The cassette is in a spring-opening panel behind Manson's desk. It is up to your people how fast they break into the deposit boxes. Assuming they enter the bank around 02.00 on Saturday morning, they should have cleared the boxes by the evening.' I paused and looked at Klaus. 'Any questions so far?'

Klaus looked at Harry who shook his head.

'You and Harry will work out the details later,' Klaus said. 'Now tell me how to get the money out.'

'At first, this seemed to me a major problem, but I've got it fixed. There are some four hundred deposit boxes in the vault. Not all of them are in use, but to make sure, your people will have to open them all. Those that are in use will contain money, jewellery, bonds and documents. You must have cartons in which to move the loot. It takes the guard around three minutes to patrol the bank before returning to his sentry-box by the bank's entrance. So your people will have to rush in, not only with the cutter, but a number of collapsible cartons. The change of guards takes place on Sunday morning at 08.00. This is when the loot must be moved. It is an acceptable risk because there are few people on the street, and the guards will be chatting each other up in front of the bank. At exactly 07.55, a security truck will arrive at the back of the bank. Every Monday morning, a security truck arrives around 08.00, delivering bank reserves, money for wages and so on. Everyone in Sharnville has seen this truck at one time or the other. You can say it is a familiar landmark.' I pointed my pencil to the blueprint. 'The truck arrives at the bank, here, and drives down this ramp into the cellar. Once in, the doors, leading into the cellar, automatically shut. The truck driver has a neutraliser that opens the door of the cellar. Once in the cellar, he waits, until one of the staff opens a steel door with direct access into the vault. This staff member will not open the steel door until the truck driver has identified himself. I can open the doors to the cellar and the steel door into the bank, but only from inside the vault. You will have to supply an identical truck and two men wearing security guards' uniform. You put the cartons in the truck and drive away. Unless your men slip up, there will be no alert until the bank opens on Monday morning so your men should get well away.'

Klaus looked at Harry.

'Can you get a truck and the uniforms?'

'Sure. I'll need to get a photo of the truck and the uniforms. I know a guy who can fix it. No problem.'

Turning to me, Klaus said, 'You think this plan of yours will succeed?'

'If it doesn't, no other plan will.' I pointed to the gimmick and to the blueprint. 'I've made it as foolproof as possible. It is now up to your people.'

'No, Mr Lucas, it will be up to you. You will be with them.' He leaned forward to stare at me, his eyes glittering. 'If anything goes wrong, you will be shot. Benny killed Marsh, and he killed Thomson. He has orders to shoot you if this operation fails or if he thinks you are being tricky. Remember that.' His face set in a snarling mask. 'And there is another thing for you to remember. I will personally shoot your woman, Mr Lucas! This operation must succeed!'

'I hear you,' I said.

Klaus looked at Harry.

'Get it moving, Harry: the truck, the uniforms, the cutter and the cartons. I want the operation to begin Saturday week at 3 a.m. You will discuss with Mr Lucas all the necessary details tomorrow night. Where will you meet him?'

Harry scratched his beard as he thought.

'Nine, tomorrow night, at the Golden Rose motel on the 'Frisco highway.' He looked at me. 'Do you know it?'

'I'll find it.'

'Ask for cabin six.' He gave a sly, cocky grin. 'They know me there.'

Getting up, he left the room.

'Are you satisfied?' I asked Klaus.

'If Harry finds no problems, I will pay you as agreed.' He took from a drawer a bulky envelope. Opening the envelope, he produced bearer bonds. 'Two hundred and fifty thousand dollars, Mr Lucas. Look at them.' He pushed the bonds across the desk. 'They should give you an incentive.'

I picked up the bonds. They were each of the value of $25,000. Ten of them: they looked as if they had passed through many hands. I put them back on the desk, and Klaus scooped them up.

'These bonds will be delivered to you at your office next week if I am satisfied Harry thinks there are no problems.'

I picked up my briefcase and got to my feet.

'No money ... no operation,' I said.

'If there are no problems, you will get the money. From what you have told me, I don't anticipate problems. When you get the bonds, be careful. If you decide to sacrifice your woman's life, and bolt, don't do it.' Once again his face turned into a snarling mask. 'From now on, you will be watched. I have an organisation: not just three men. If you try to bolt, you won't get far, and your end will be unpleasant.' The slate-grey eyes lit up. 'They will cut off your hands, blind you and cut off your tongue. You will be left to bleed to death. So don't try anything tricky, Mr Lucas.'

Then I knew he was utterly mad.

'I hear you,' I said, and leaving him, I walked into the lobby. Benny, standing by the front door, sneered at me.

'Be seeing you, fink,' he said.

I went out to where Joe, playing his harmonica, sat in the Chevvy.

As I slid, into the passenger's seat, I thought thankfully that Klaus wasn't as smart as Joe said he was. I had taken a risk. Neither Klaus, Harry nor Joe had an idea that I had a tape recorder built into the lid of my briefcase, and I now had a tape recording of every word they had said.

Joe sat silent as he drove down to the highway. I glanced at him, seeing his black sweating face dimly lit by the dashboard lights. He looked, as I hoped he would look, like a man with a load on his mind. When we reached the highway, and were heading towards Sharnville, I said,

'Your boss, Joe, is happy. We break into the bank at three o'clock Saturday morning.'

He grunted, the worried frown on his face deepened, but he still said nothing.

It wasn't until we were nearing my apartment block that I said, 'Come on in, and have a drink with me, Joe, or have you a date?'

He stared at me for a brief moment. I could see the whites of his eyes.

'You asking me to drink with you, Mr Lucas?' There was surprise in his voice.

'Look, Joe, we are all in this. With luck, we're all going to be rich.' I underlined the word *luck*. 'Cut out this crap, don't call me mister ... call me Larry.'

He pulled up outside my apartment block.

'Harry has never asked me to drink with him,' he muttered.

'Oh, come on, Joe.' I got out of the car. 'Don't act like an Uncle Tom.'

I walked across the sidewalk, willing him to follow me. As I was pushing open the glass door to the lobby, he joined me. We rode up in the elevator. I unlocked my front door and moved aside to let him pass. He stood uneasily while I shut and locked the door.

'Whisky and Coke, okay?' I said, going over to the liquor cabinet.

'Yeah, man.' He looked around the room, wiping sweat off his face with the back of his hand. 'I don't catch this. What do you want to give me a drink for?'

'Quit being servile, Joe,' I said impatiently. 'You're a man like I am, and we're going to work together. Sit down, for Christ's sake!'

Muttering to himself, he sat down in an armchair, resting his elbows on his knees.

I fixed him a drink that could have knocked over a mule. Keeping my back turned, I poured myself a Coke and left out the whisky. I gave him his drink and sat down, opposite him.

Speaking casually, I told him how we would break into the bank, all about the gimmicks and the neutralisers, how Harry was fixing the getaway truck. I gave him all the details, and he sat forward, his black face intent, listening, while he kept sipping his drink.

'So that's it, Joe,' I concluded, noticing by now his glass was nearly empty. 'With luck, by next Monday morning, you will be rich.'

His eyes narrowed.

'Didn't I tell you, man, I'm never lucky? I've been thinking about what you said. I'm not even sure of Harry now.'

'Oh, come on, Joe. You said you could trust Harry.'

'Yeah.' He finished his drink and grimaced. 'Harry and me shared a cell for three years. That's a mighty long time. We got along fine together. He fixed me up with the boss.'

'What was he in for, Joe?'

'Harry? His old man was the finest forger of bonds ever. Harry handled them. Harry told me his old man got careless, and they caught him and Harry. Harry drew six years.'

The finest forger of bonds!

The nickel dropped.

I realised why Klaus had agreed to pay me in bonds. I was now sure the bonds he had shown me had been forged by Harry's father!

Looking at Joe, I could see the drink was hitting him. There was now a dazed look in his eyes, and he kept rubbing his mouth aimlessly with the back of his hand.

'Harry seems okay with me,' I said, 'but Benny scares me. I get a feeling once the money is in the truck, he's going to kill me. He could kill you and Harry too.'

Joe shook his head as if trying to clear it. He stared at me.

'Yeah, man. I don't dig Benny.'

'Have you a gun, Joe?'

'Sure, I've got a gun.'

'I wish to God I had one. Together – you and I – could take care of Benny if he started something.'

Joe gaped at me.

'What's that mean, man?'

'Neither of us need worry about Benny if I had a gun. I could watch him when you're doing the work, and you could watch him while I was doing the work.'

He screwed up his eyes while he thought.

'But Harry would be watching him.'

'I'm going to talk to Harry, Joe. With the three of us watching Benny, he won't stand a chance of double-crossing us.'

He thought some more, then nodded.

'Yeah, that's right.' He reached in his hip pocket and produced a .38 police special. 'You have this, man. I've got another in my pad. Yeah, between the three of us, we can handle Benny.'

I took the gun, not quite believing it would be as easy as this.

'Another thing, Joe: don't entirely trust Harry. That's a lot of money. Harry could knock Benny off. He could also knock both of us off.'

Joe again screwed up his eyes, then shook his head.

'I don't dig that ... not Harry.'

'It's a lot of money.'

He thought some more, then nodded.

'Yeah, it sure is.'

'Look, Joe, it's up to you to take care of yourself. Three million dollars! You've got to be sure you get your share. I

97

have no worry. As I told you, I'm getting my cut in advance, but you have to worry about Benny and Harry. I'll watch you, and you watch me. Don't say anything to Harry. You just never know.'

'Yeah.' He shook his head. 'Who the hell knows? You know something, man? I've drunk too much.' He got unsteadily to his feet. 'I'm going back to my pad.'

'Do you want me to drive you, Joe?'

He lurched to the door, paused and looked at me.

'Would you?'

'We're working together, Joe. I don't want some smart cop picking you up. I'll drive you home.'

'Thanks, man. I guess that drink …'

I steered him to the elevator and down to the Chevvy.

'Where do we go?' I asked, as we settled in the car.

'Straight ahead. Tenth to the right. No. 45,' he mumbled, as his head fell forward.

After a ten minute drive, I stopped outside a walk-up apartment block and shook him awake.

'We're here, Joe.'

He pawed my arm.

'You're a real pal, man,' he muttered. 'You take the car back. I'll pick it up tomorrow. Man! Was that drink strong!'

As he made to get out of the car, I caught hold of his arm.

'Joe … where is Glenda?'

He stared drunkenly at me.

'With the boss, man. Where do you think? All nice and snug with Benny breathing down her neck.'

He reeled out of the car and plodded across the sidewalk. I watched him open the front door and disappear. Then I drew in a long, deep breath.

It seemed to me the cards were falling my way.

'The truck will be ready next week,' Harry said. 'I've got the uniforms fixed.'

We were sitting in cabin six at the Golden Rose motel. The room was comfortably furnished with a double bed against the far wall, four lounging chairs, a TV set and a liquor cabinet. We were both nursing whiskys as we sat opposite each other.

'I'll collect the truck around midnight from 'Frisco,' Harry went on. 'That's no problem. I have a couple of stooges who will be the guards.'

'They know what they are walking into?' I asked.

'Oh, sure. They're picking up a couple of grand. For that money, they would cut their mothers' throats.' He eyed me thoughtfully. 'The one weak thing in this operation is this patrolling guard. How would it be if we knocked him off, and put a guy in his place?'

This suggestion shocked me, but it warned me that Harry was as ruthless as Klaus.

'The guard is relieved Sunday morning. Get rid of him, and the operation is blown.'

Harry thought about this, then nodded.

'Yep. I see that.' He scratched at his beard, then smiled. He said he had a girlfriend who would be waiting on the east side of the bank, and when the guard came around, out of sight of the bank's entrance, she would ask him to direct her to a hotel.

'She's cute,' Harry said, his grin widening. 'She can chat up this guard for at least five minutes: all the time we need to get into the bank. She's done jobs for me before, and she's sharp.'

This seemed to me a sound idea. I had been worrying about the guard.

'I go along with that,' I said. 'Now tell me, pal is this shindig going to work?'

'My end will. What happens when you get the loot into the truck and take off is up to you.'

He regarded me, his eyes narrowing. 'Why shouldn't we get the money away? You said the alert won't be until Monday morning. That gives us all Sunday to get lost.'

'That's fine.' I sipped my drink. 'Then you have no problem, but that's a lot of money.'

He cocked his head on one side.

'So?'

'You realise Klaus is as nutty as a fruitcake? He's a psychopath.'

'Suppose he is?'

'Three million, Harry. Even a psychopath doesn't give that kind of money away. You're talking all the risks. He just sits back.'

He stiffened and leaned forward.

'So?'

'Anything. I don't have to worry. I'm being paid in advance. It's you who have to worry.'

'You think Klaus could double-cross us?' There was a note of uncertainty in his voice.

'You are dealing with a nut case. Anything can happen. I don't know. He might be so nutty he will let you three walk away with three million dollars. On the other hand he might arrange for you and Joe to get knocked off, and take the money for himself.'

Harry scratched his beard, his eyes uneasy.

'Who would knock us off?'

'He tells me he has an organisation.'

Harry laughed.

'Sure: he has me, Joe and Benny: that's his organisation. He likes to talk big. I'm the guy who knows where to hire help: he doesn't. You're talking a load of crap. Once we get the money, there's nothing he can do about it.'

'There's Benny,' I said quietly.

Harry jerked upright. He looked like a man who had walked into a brick wall.

'Yeah ... there's Benny.' He sat silent, thinking, as he stared into his glass.

'Benny is a moronic killer,' I said. 'If you can trust him, you have no problem. I wouldn't trust him further than I can throw him. He bothers me. Given the slightest chance, I think he would knock off the three of us, and drive away with the loot. That's my thinking.'

Harry shifted uneasily. He thought about this, frowning, then finally he said, 'Aw, come on. I ...'

'What would a moron like Benny do with three million dollars?' I broke in. 'If he knocked off the three of us, he wouldn't know how to handle money that big, but Klaus would. Benny would go to Klaus. Maybe Klaus has already sold him on the idea. He'll tell him how to handle the money. So Benny could be a sucker too. What's to stop Klaus knocking Benny off, and vanishing with the money? Three million dollars!'

Harry stared at me, and I could see I had got him worried.

'You're a smart guy,' he said slowly. 'You've given me something to think about. You do your job, and leave me to look after Benny. Now let's go over the whole operation from A to Z. Right?'

Certain I had sown a seed of doubt in his mind, I produced the blueprint of the bank from my briefcase, and for the next two hours, we worked on the break-in.

Harry was quick and intelligent. His questions were probing, but he seemed satisfied with my answers.

Finally, he said, 'That's it. It looks good to me.'

'Sure?'

'Can't see how it can go wrong. Yeah, it's fine.'

'Tell Klaus that. He's agreed to pay me in advance if you're satisfied.'

He gave me a sly look.

'Looking after yourself, huh?'

'I'd be a sucker if I didn't. I'm not kidding myself you three would share with me. My share comes out of Klaus' pocket.'

'What's he paying you?'

'Two hundred and fifty thousand in bearer bonds.'

I saw his eyes shift.

'Bearer bonds?' he repeated.

'Yes ... as good as cash.'

He gave me a sly little grin that told me all I wanted to know. He knew the bonds Klaus had given me were forgeries.

'You're real smart.' He nodded. 'Bonds are a lot better than a heap of bills.'

'They sure are,' I said, thinking, okay, you twister, my laugh will come last. 'How are you getting rid of the jewellery?' I went on casually as I put the blueprint back in my briefcase. 'There'll be a lot of it.'

'Should be no problem. I've a guy lined up who'll handle it, but there will be cash, won't there?'

'Yes, but more jewellery than cash.' He grimaced.

'You think there's three million in that vault?'

'I don't know: could be more. In a town as rich as Sharnville, there must be a lot of money stashed away in the vault. There are all kinds of big property deals going on right now, and a lot of it will be in cash to avoid tax.'

'Okay. Well, I guess that fixes it.' He got to his feet. 'A real nice operation. Klaus may be a nut case, but he's certainly smart.'

'So Joe tells me.'

'We'll pick you up at your place at 2.30 next Sunday morning. Right?'

'I'll be ready.'

'And if something turns up, I'll give you a call at your office.'

'Give your name as Benson, and say you're from IBM.'

'Right.'

As we moved to the door, I said, 'And watch Benny.'

'I'll watch him.' He paused and stared at me, his eyes suddenly cold. 'And I'll watch you too, buster.'

Moving by me, he walked out into the darkness to the Chevvy. As he drove away, I turned off the stop switch of the tape recorder, concealed in the handle of my briefcase.

I went over to my car, put the briefcase carefully on the passenger's seat and headed back to my apartment.

Around 11.00 on Wednesday morning, as I put down the telephone receiver after a long call from Bill Dixon, my secretary came in.

'A special delivery for you, Mr Lucas. It's marked personal.' She put a bulky envelope on my desk.

'Thanks, Mary.'

I waited until she had left, then picking up the envelope by one corner, I carefully slit the flat. The bonds spilled out. I regarded them. They looked genuine enough, but I wasn't fooled. There was no note. Using my handkerchief, I put the bonds back into the envelope, and locked the envelope in one of my desk drawers.

I sat back and considered my position. I had two damning tapes covering Klaus' talk with me, and Harry's talk with me. I also had Joe on tape. I had Harry's fingerprints on my briefcase. It had been a stroke of luck that he had snatched the briefcase from me as I was about to open it. His prints would be on record. With any luck, Klaus' prints would be on the envelope and possibly, the bonds. With his record, the forged bonds would get Klaus a long term in jail. I could tie him, Harry and Joe in with the break-in, but not Benny. That bothered me. So far, I had nothing on Benny. Then Mary looked in to say the building contractor was waiting to see me, and for the next three hours, I was all business.

Around 13.00, my usual lunchtime, I told Mary I had a special job to do and to send out for sandwiches for me.

'I need another tape recorder, Mary. I want to copy some tapes.'

'I'll do that for you, Mr Lucas.'

'Thanks, but I'll do it myself. For the next hour, don't put any telephone calls through: say I'm out to lunch.'

Taking the recorder from her, I locked my office door, and made a copy of the two tapes. Then using my portable typewriter I wrote, in duplicate, to Farrell Brannigan. I told him of my love for Glenda, of Klaus and his blackmail, and of his determination to break into the safest bank in the world. I told him there was enough on the tapes to nail Klaus, and that the bonds he had given me were forgeries. I omitted no details. I ended by telling him Klaus was threatening to kill Glenda and myself if the bank break-in failed.

I read through the statement, then satisfied, I put it in an envelope, together with the original tapes and sealed the envelope. I locked the copy of my statement with the tape copies in my desk drawer. By then it was 14.15, and I could hear Mary moving around in her office. I unlocked my office door and told her I was ready for business, and a few minutes later the telephone bell began to ring.

It wasn't until after 20.00, when Mary and the rest of the staff had long gone and I had cleared my desk, that I was once again able to concentrate on the problem facing me. I was now satisfied that I had taken care of myself, but not Glenda. Somehow, I had to get her away from Klaus. According to Joe, she was a prisoner in Klaus' place. At least, I told myself I had all day Thursday and Friday to fix something.

Taking the original tapes and my statement, leaving the copies in my desk drawer, I went down to my car. I had put the gun Joe had given me in the glove compartment of my car. As I started the engine, I took the gun and dropped it into my jacket pocket. It gave me a feeling of security. I parked some two hundred yards from my apartment block. I was now taking no chances. Carrying the bulky envelope containing the tapes and my statement, my hand resting on the butt of the gun, I walked into the lighted entrance. As I neared the glass doors leading into the lighted lobby, I paused, looking right and left, then I started forward again, but immediately stopped.

Sitting in one of the lounging chairs in the lobby, by the elevator, his hat at the back of his head, a racing sheet in his hand, was Benny.

The sight of him sent a chill up my spine. I spun around, and moving fast, I headed back to my car. Obviously, Benny was waiting for me, but why? Seeing the bulky envelope I was carrying, he might grab it. I wasn't ready yet for a showdown with Klaus.

How long would Benny wait for me? I wanted to get to my apartment, but I had to wait until he had gone. I decided I would drive to a restaurant at the end of the street, have dinner and then make a cautious return.

As I paused by my car, I saw Deputy Sheriff Fred Maclain, now acting sheriff of Sharnville, walking along the sidewalk towards me.

'Hi, there, Fred!'

He paused, peered at me, then his red, bloated face split into a grin.

'Hi, Mr Lucas.'

I shook his hand.

'Terrible thing about Joe,' I said. 'I can't get him off my mind.'

'Yeah.' Maclain blew out his fat cheeks. 'We'll get the punk, Mr Lucas. Don't worry about that. We'll get him!'

'I'm sure you will, Fred.' I paused, then went on, 'I'm just going up to my apartment for a quick snort. Then, I have a dinner date. Feel like joining me? I've got some good Scotch.'

'It's bad luck to refuse a drink, Mr Lucas,' he said, grinning. 'Lead me to it.'

We walked back together, and into the apartment block's lobby. Out of the corner of my eye, I saw Benny stiffen, start to get to his feet, then seeing Maclain, he resettled himself in his chair, staring at the racing sheet. I led Maclain to the elevator, not looking at Benny. I saw Maclain staring at Benny, his little pig eyes hardening.

'Just a moment, Mr Lucas,' and he walked over to Benny. 'Haven't seen you around here before, stranger,' he said, in his rough cop voice. 'I'm sheriff here. I like to check strange faces. Who are you?'

Benny got hastily to his feet. His brutal face shone with sweat.

'Just resting my dogs,' he said. 'Any harm in that?'

'You live here?' Maclain barked. He was only happy when he was barking at people.

'No ... just resting my dogs.'

'Then rest your goddamn feet some place else. What's your name, and where do you come from?'

'Tom Schultz,' Benny said, backing away. 'I've got an hour to wait for my train.'

'Come on, Fred,' I said. 'Time's running out.'

Maclain grunted, then waved Benny to the door.

'Get lost,' he said, and as Benny walked out into the night, Maclain grinned, then joined me at the elevator.

'He looked a punk,' he said, as we entered the elevator. 'I hate punks.'

In my apartment, I built him a whisky and soda, and got him settled in a lounging chair.

'Excuse me for a moment, Fred,' I said. 'I want to wash up.'

'You go ahead.' He sipped the whisky and sighed. 'Now that's what I call the genuine stuff.'

I put the bottle and charge water on a table by his side, then I went into my bedroom. I put the envelope into a briefcase which I had already wrapped in cellophane. Going into the kitchen, I found a sheet of brown paper and string and made a parcel of the briefcase. All this took less than fifteen minutes.

Carrying the parcel, I returned to the living-room. Maclain was humming softly. I saw the level in the whisky bottle had shrunk.

'Damn fine whisky, Mr Lucas.'

I went to my desk and addressed the parcel to Brannigan at the Californian National Bank, Los Angeles.

'Can I ask a favour, Fred?'

He blinked blearily at me.

'For you. Sure ... anything.'

107

He poured more whisky into his glass, drank, sighed and shook his head in appreciation.

'I have here in this parcel some important papers for Mr Brannigan,' I said, hoping he wasn't, by now, too drunk to understand. 'Would you lock this parcel in your safe, Fred?'

He gaped at me.

'Put it in the bank, Mr Lucas.'

'I told Mr Brannigan I would give the parcel to you for safe-keeping,' I said. 'He went along with the idea. He thinks a lot of you, Fred. He told me you would be the next sheriff if he has anything to do with it, and you know Mr Brannigan draws a lot of water.'

Maclain's bloated face lit up with a delighted grin.

'He said that? Mr Brannigan?'

'That's what he said.'

'Yeah, and he's right.' He levered himself out of his chair. 'For Mr Brannigan, any favour.'

'I want you to keep this parcel in your safe, Fred. If you don't hear from me on Monday morning, I want you to deliver this parcel in person to Mr Brannigan. Monday morning after ten o'clock, and not before. Now listen, Fred, this parcel is important. When you drive to Los Angeles, take one of your boys with you. Mr Brannigan would appreciate this, and don't give this parcel to anyone except Mr Brannigan.'

Maclain gaped at me.

'Well, okay. I'll take care of it. On Monday morning, huh?'

'That's it. When Mr Brannigan gets this parcel, you can reckon on becoming the sheriff of Sharnville.'

He hitched up his gun belt, pushed his Stetson hat to the back of his head and grinned drunkenly at me.

'Consider it done, Mr Lucas.'

'Thanks, Fred. Let's go. I'll drive you back. I want to see this parcel locked in your safe.'

'Sure.' He bent forward and splashed more whisky into his glass, drank the whisky, grunted, grinned at me, then holding the parcel under his arm, he went with me to the elevator.

At the police station, I watched him lock the parcel in the big safe.

'Okay, Fred, unless you hear from me before ten o'clock on Monday, take this parcel with an escort to Mr Brannigan.'

'Sure, Mr Lucas. I'll take care of it.' He wiped his lips with the back of his hand. 'That was fine whisky.'

I left him and returned to my car.

Sitting in the passenger's seat, his hat at the back of his head, was Benny.

6

'Hi fink,' Benny said, grinning evilly. 'The boss wants you. Let's move.'

'I'll see him tomorrow night at nine,' I said. 'Now, get out!'

'You'll see him right now, fink, or I'll start breaking your whore's fingers. Let's move.'

I placed my hand on the horn button.

'Listen to me, Benny, you touch her, and the operation is off. I'll see Klaus tomorrow night, and not before. Get out or I'll start the horn, and you'll get a load of law in your lap.'

We stared at each other. There was an uneasy, frustrated rage in his eyes.

'Get out!' I repeated.

'I told the boss you'd be a smart sonofabitch, but don't kid yourself, fink, I'll take care of you.'

At this moment, a patrolman came out of the station house. He paused, then came over to my car.

'Evening, Mr Lucas,' he said. 'You can't park here.'

'Hi, Tom.' I knew most of the patrolmen. 'I'm on my way.' Turning to Benny, I said, 'Then tomorrow. So long.'

Benny hesitated, then aware that the patrolman was staring at him, he slid out of the car and walked across the street.

'Who's he?' the patrolman asked. 'I haven't seen him around.'

'Business, Tom.' I forced a smile. 'They come in all shapes and sizes,' then nodding, I drove down the street. I stopped outside a Howard Johnson restaurant and went in. I ordered a club sandwich, and while I ate it, I thought about Glenda. She was now very much on my mind. I felt that I had enough on Klaus not only to stop the break-in but to get Glenda away from him. With the evidence I had given Maclain to guard, I was sure I had Klaus trapped. I couldn't see how he could wriggle out of it. I knew I was taking a risk, dealing with a psychopath, but it seemed to me he would either have to accept defeat or eventually be jailed for years once Brannigan and the police came after him.

I spent a restless night, half sleeping, half dozing. I kept thinking of Glenda, and the more I thought of her, the more I realised how much she meant to me. If I could call Klaus' bluff, stop the bank break-in, make him leave Sharnville, then my life would once again be on an even keel. Now Marsh was dead, there was nothing to stop me marrying Glenda, always providing Klaus disappeared.

I was glad I had so much office work to do the following day. The rush of work prevented me worrying about the evening when I had to face Klaus. In the afternoon, Bill Dixon phoned through to say he had landed another contract to build a small factory to produce electrical components, and they wanted office furniture. Could I see the director on Monday to discuss exactly what he wanted? I said there would be no problem, and fixed a time. As I hung up I wondered if I would still be in Sharnville on Monday. If I couldn't bluff Klaus, then I would be on the run.

I considered writing a letter to Bill Dixon, enclosing a copy of my statement to Brannigan in case I had to get out fast, but I decided I had all day Friday and half Friday night to decide which way the dice would fall.

If I were forced to go on the run, I would need cash. I checked my bank statement. I had some eight thousand dollars in my account. I wrote a cheque for this amount, then telling Mary I was going to the bank and would be back right away, I left my office.

As I was waiting for the traffic lights to change, I spotted Joe, propping up a fire hydrant. He and I looked at each other, then the lights changed and I crossed. I went into the lobby of the bank, signed my name with a computer pen, fed the cheque into the slot, and after a minute or so, the money dropped into a pay-out slot. I put the bills into my hip pocket and returned to my office block. Joe was still propping up the fire hydrant. I ignored him, pushed open the glass doors and took the elevator up to my office.

I spent the rest of the day clearing my desk. There was a mass of outstanding work still to be done, and if I had to bolt, I didn't want Bill to be landed with too much work.

At 19.00, I told Mary to go home. When she had gone, I put the copy of my statement to Brannigan and the two tapes into my briefcase. Then picking up a small tape player, I locked up and went down to my car.

As I was unlocking the car door, Joe materialised out of the shadows.

'You seeing the boss tonight, Mr Lucas?' There was an anxious note in his voice.

'I'm seeing him, Joe,' I said. 'You don't have to hang around me. I'll be there at nine.'

'The boss told me to keep tabs on you, Mr Lucas. I do what I'm told.'

'I'm going to have dinner. Come with me,' I said, and got in my car. Leaning over, I unlocked the passenger's door.

Joe gaped at me.

'I can't eat with you.'

'Oh, skip it, Joe. I know a place. You may as well eat if you have to keep tabs on me.'

He hesitated, then got in beside me.

I drove to a small restaurant that employed black staff. The restaurant was noted for its steaks, and I often ate there.

Joe seemed to relax as he settled himself at a corner table. There were more blacks than whites at the tables, and the black waiter gave him a friendly smile.

'Two steaks, rare,' I said, 'and beers.'

I took out a pack of cigarettes and offered it to Joe who shook his head.

'I don't smoke, Mr Lucas.'

As I lit up, I said, 'Time's running out, Joe. Are you still going ahead with it?'

He moved uneasily.

'Like you, Mr Lucas, I've got to do what I'm told.'

'You don't. You can get on a bus and disappear.'

He stared at me.

'Why should I do that?'

'Better to disappear than get a bullet through your head.'

He flinched.

'You said Harry, you and me would watch Benny.'

'I've talked to Harry. He's worrying about himself. He's not worrying about you, Joe. I can understand that. I'm worrying about myself.'

The steaks arrived with the beer. I began to eat my steak, but Joe sat still, staring down at his plate, his face creased in a worried frown.

'Come on, Joe, eat up,' I said. 'I could be wrong about Benny, but if I were black, I would get the hell out of Sharnville. I would rather have my life than risk Benny.'

'I've no place to go,' he muttered. 'I've got no money.'

While his mind was occupied with his troubles, I shot out, 'How's Miss Glenda, Joe?'

Off-guard, he looked up.

'She's having it rough, Mr Lucas. That Benny ...' Then he stopped short.

I stiffened.

'What's Benny doing to her, Joe?'

He began to toy with his steak.

'You see, Mr Lucas, I don't hang around the place nor does Harry, but Benny stays there all the time. He's the boss' bodyguard. He's got nothing to do but to pester Miss Glenda, and he sure does.'

'You realise your boss has kidnapped her, Joe?'

He chewed on his steak while he thought about this, then he shook his head.

'That ain't right, Mr Lucas. She works for him.'

'She has been forced to work for him, and she is being held prisoner. In law, Joe, that makes your boss, you, Harry, and Benny kidnappers. You get a much longer stretch for kidnapping than for breaking into a bank.'

His eyes shifted.

'I know nothing about the law,' he mumbled. 'I do what I'm told ... like you. I've got to.'

'Would you help me free her, Joe?'

His eyes grew round.

'The boss wouldn't dig that, Mr Lucas.'

'Never mind about him, think of yourself. If you helped me to get her free, you wouldn't go to jail as a kidnapper.'

'How would I help you?' he asked, and cut another piece of steak.

'Is Harry out there tonight?'

'He's gone to 'Frisco about the truck.'

'So there's only Benny, your boss and Miss Glenda there?'

He nodded.

'Do you know where she is, Joe?'

'Sure. She's in a room at the back of the house.'

'Is the door locked?'

'Not locked: it's bolted on the outside.'

I pushed aside my plate. Then taking out the bills I had drawn from the bank, keeping them out of sight under the table, I peeled off five one-thousand dollar bills. The rest of the money I put back in my pocket.

'The bank operation is off, Joe,' I said. 'Don't ask questions: take it from me it is off. Here's your chance to get away. I'll give you five thousand dollars if you'll get Miss Glenda out of that house.'

His eyes bugged out.

'Five thousand bucks?' He put down his knife and fork and stared at me. 'You'll give me five thousand bucks?'

There was no one sitting at the tables near us, so I showed him the bills. He gaped at them.

'Now, listen, Joe. It's easy. This is what you do. I'll drive you out to the house and leave you at the end of the lane. While I'm talking to Klaus, you get in, go to Miss Glenda's room, get her out and put her in my car. Drive her to the Sherwood Hotel and leave her there. Tell her I'll join her later. That's all you have to do. Then drive back, leave my car by the gate, then beat it. At the highway, you can get a bus. With five thousand dollars you can get lost. You won't have to worry about a kidnapping rap nor being arrested for trying to break into the bank. What do you say?'

He screwed up his eyes while he thought. I waited, my hands clammy, my heart thumping. Finally, he shook his head.

'There's three million in that bank. Five grand is peanuts.'

'Don't be a fool, Joe! I've told you there's not going to be a break-in.' I picked up my briefcase, standing on the floor

115

by my side, took out my statement to Brannigan and handed it to him.

'Read that.'

It took him nearly ten minutes to read the statement. He traced each word with a thick finger, frowning, and holding the two sheets of paper close to his face as if he were short-sighted. Finally, he finished, then stared at me.

'The boss will kill you, Mr Lucas.'

'No, he won't. A copy is already in the hands of the police. They read it on Monday morning and they will go into action. They have the forged bonds with Klaus' prints on them. By this time tomorrow, Joe, he'll be miles away, and he won't be worrying about you.'

'You mention me in this,' Joe said, tapping the statement.

'But no description, Joe. If you free Miss Glenda, with this money, you haven't a care in the world.'

Again he screwed up his eyes while he thought.

'You sure played it smart, Mr Lucas. Yeah. I've thought about what you said the other night. I can't imagine Benny letting me walk away with a big lump of money even if we did get into the bank. Yeah, I guess I'd be smart to play along with you.'

I drew in a long, deep breath.

All my nights of thinking had paid off!

'So you'll get her out, Joe, and take her to the Sherwood Hotel?'

'Yeah. That's what I'll do. Then I'll bring your car back and get me out of Sharnville pronto.'

I studied his black, sweating face. I felt I could trust him.

'Don't worry about Benny. I'll get him in the room with Klaus. Give me exactly ten minutes from the time I enter the house. Have you a watch?'

'Sure, Mr Lucas.'

'I'll make sure the front door is unlocked. Give me ten minutes, then get Miss Glenda out. Understand?'

'Sure ... ten minutes, and I get her out.'

'Right.' I looked at my watch. I had twenty minutes now to get to Klaus' place by 21.00. I called for the bill, paid, then picking up my briefcase, I went out to my car, closely followed by Joe. We got in the car, and I headed out of town.

Joe said, 'When do I get the money, Mr Lucas?'

'I'll explain that.'

We said nothing until we reached the dirt road leading to Klaus' place. Halfway up the dirt road, I stopped the car.

'Now about the money.' I took the bills from my pocket, folded them in half, then carefully tore them apart.

'Hey, Mr Lucas! What's that you are doing?' Joe's voice shot up.

I handed him the torn half of the five bills and put the other half in my pocket.

'The moment I know Miss Glenda is at the Sherwood Hotel, Joe, I will deliver the other half to you ... no problem. I just want to make sure you don't chicken out. Okay?'

'You'll bring them to my pad?'

'That's it. When I'm through with your boss, I'll drive to the Sherwood Hotel, see Miss Glenda, then come on to you. You stick the bills together and get lost.'

He nodded.

'Okay, Mr Lucas.'

We got out of the car and walked up the road. It was now dark. I could see the lights were on in the house.

'Well, see you at your pad, Joe,' I said. 'I'll take came of Benny. You have nothing to worry about. You get Miss Glenda to the Sherwood Hotel.' I caught hold of his damp hand and shook it. 'Give me ten minutes from now.'

'Sure, Mr Lucas.'

I walked quickly up to the gate, pushed it open and walked to the front door. My heart was hammering and my mouth was dry. As I rang the doorbell, my hand pulled out the gun Joe had given me.

Benny opened the door.

'Come on in, fink,' he said.

As I stepped into the lighted lobby, I lifted the gun and shoved it hard against his fat belly.

'Don't take chances, Benny,' I said quietly. 'I'm longing to put a bullet in your guts. Take me to Klaus.'

Benny stared down at the gun, his brutal face expressionless. Then moving carefully, he walked ahead of me and into the living-room.

Klaus was sitting at his desk. His ice-grey eyes regarded me as I closed the door.

'The fink's got a gun,' Benny said.

Klaus' expression didn't change.

'Get over there, against the far wall,' I said to Benny, 'and stay there.'

Benny grinned.

'Anything you say, fink,' and he crossed the room to the wall behind Klaus, and he rested his heavy shoulders against the wall.

Klaus said, 'A gun, Mr Lucas? So you have decided to be tricky. That is regrettable. Now, you are going to tell me the operation is off.'

'Correct.' I put the briefcase and the tape player on his desk. Using my left hand, still pointing the gun between Klaus and Benny, I opened the briefcase, took out my statement to Brannigan and slid it across the desk. 'Read that.'

Klaus picked up the statement and read it. Then he looked up.

118

'A masterpiece of brevity, Mr Lucas.' I had expected a violent reaction, and this relaxed remark made me uneasy.

'The bonds you sent me are forgeries,' I said. 'Here are two tapes I want you to listen to. They will convince you the break-in is off.'

I put the tape on the player and turned the player on. For two or three minutes, Klaus listened to his own voice. When my voice said, *Did you have to murder Sheriff Thomson?* and he replied, *Let that be an example to you. When anyone obstructs me or is likely to obstruct me, I get rid of him*, he leaned forward and pressed the stop button.

'I'll take the rest as read,' he said, and sat back.

'Copies of these statements and the tapes are with the police,' I said, and glanced at my watch. I had been in the room for fifteen minutes. By now, Glenda would be driving with Joe to the Sherwood Hotel. 'I have arranged for the statement and the tapes to be delivered by the police to Brannigan on Monday morning. If anything happens to me, Brannigan will have enough to nail you, Klaus. That's why I am telling you the break-in is off.'

'Why should anything happen to you, Mr Lucas?' Klaus lifted his eyebrows. 'If anything is going to happen, then it will happen to your woman. You are far too important to me to harm.'

'By now, Klaus, Glenda is out of your reach.'

He gave a little chuckle that sent a chill up my spine.

'First, let me congratulate you, Mr Lucas. You made an excellent try.' He waved to the statement and the tape player. 'All very efficient, and well thought out, but unhappily for you, you are an amateur dealing with a professional. At three o'clock on Saturday morning, you will supervise the bank break-in. Make no mistake about that!'

I stared at him, feeling a gradual and deadly loss of confidence.

'You are wrong. You now know the situation. Your sick idea isn't going to work. Take my advice: get out of Sharnville before Brannigan puts you in jail.'

'So you imagine Glenda is out of my reach?' He shook his head. 'She is locked in her room. I think you are romancing, Mr Lucas.'

It was twenty-five minutes since I had been in the house. By now, Glenda would be safe in the Sherwood Hotel.

Then I heard a sound that froze me: the mournful spiritual, played on a harmonica.

'There's Joe,' Klaus said, and chuckled. 'Mr Lucas, don't wave that gun about. You don't imagine I would let Joe give you a loaded gun? You see, the trouble with an amateur is that he doesn't check like a professional does. The amateur is given a gun, and he jumps to the wrong conclusion that it is loaded. Shoot at me to convince yourself.'

Grinning evilly, Benny started across the room towards me. I lifted the gun, but I couldn't bring myself to pull the trigger. I knew that I had been outwitted.

'I owe you this, fink,' Benny snarled, and his enormous fist smashed against the side of my face. A bright light exploded inside my head as I crashed to the floor. For some moments, I swam in darkness, then very faintly I heard Klaus say, 'You shouldn't have done that, Benny. There's no need for violence.'

Then I became aware of hands digging into my jacket pocket. I made a feeble effort to push the hands away as I struggled back to consciousness. There was a long pause. My head began to clear, and my face began to ache. I rolled over, then dragged myself to my knees. The room swam into focus. I saw Joe standing by the desk.

I heard him say, 'The sucker gave me five grand, boss. He tore the bills in half. I've got the other half now. Can I keep the money?'

'Of course, Joe. I would say you earned it.'

I heard Joe giggle. The sound told me that all my work on him had been wasted. Glenda was still a prisoner!

Slowly, I got to my feet, moved to a chair and sat down.

'Give Mr Lucas a drink,' Klaus said. 'He looks as if he could do with it.'

A glass of whisky was thrust into my hand.

'I apologise, Mr Lucas,' Klaus said. 'Benny gets carried away.'

I turned and threw the whisky in Benny's sneering face. He yelled, his hands going to his eyes and he staggered back. Then wiping his eyes with the backs of his hand, he started toward me, his brutal face a mask of snarling rage.

'Benny.' Klaus didn't raise his voice. 'Go and see Glenda.'

Benny paused in his rush, stopped, looked at me, then grinned.

'Yeah.'

He started to the door.

I forced myself to my feet and staggered after him. My head was raging with pain and the floor seemed tilted. Joe moved swiftly, caught hold of my arm, swung me around and slapped me hard across my mouth, then he flung me back in the chair.

Dazed, I again tried to stand up. Again Joe slammed me back. Then I heard a long, piercing scream somewhere at the back of the house: a woman's scream, and I knew it was Glenda.

'You'd better stop him, Joe,' Klaus said mildly. 'He doesn't know his own strength.'

Grinning, Joe slipped out of the room.

'It's all right, Mr Lucas,' Klaus said. 'She won't be hurt again unless, of course, you don't co-operate.'

I remembered what Glenda had said about her husband: *all his guts, and he had lots of guts, drained out of him. They took Alex's guts from him like a surgeon takes out an appendix.*

Hearing that piercing scream took all the guts I had ever had from me.

'I'll co-operate,' I said in a harsh whisper.

Joe and Benny came into the room. Benny was grinning. Joe was sweating and shaking his head.

'Well now, Mr Lucas,' Klaus said. 'Tomorrow morning you will get this statement of yours and the tapes back from the police. Is that understood?'

I nodded.

'Good. You will bring them here. Is that understood?'

Again I nodded.

He leaned forward, his face a snarling mask, his eyes blazing.

'If you try any further trickery, your woman will be tortured to death! I know all about your futile attempts to undermine Harry and Joe. There are three million dollars in that vault, and they want them! From now on you co-operate! Understood?'

'Yes.'

'Then tomorrow morning here!' He slammed his fist on the desk and screamed at me in a mad, high-pitched voice, 'No one, least of all you, will stop me breaking into that bank! Now get out!'

Joe came over to me and caught hold of my arm.

'Come on, man,' he said giggling. 'Didn't I take you for a ride!'

I pulled away from him and looked straight at him.

'And you'll regret this, Joe,' I said. 'I'm not the only one who'll be taken for a ride.'

Joe burst out laughing, slapping his great black hands on his thighs.

'Man! You sure do flap with your mouth.'

I walked out of the house to where my car was parked. As I got under the steering wheel, I remembered what Glenda had said: *He's a devil*.

I felt utterly defeated and crushed. The trap had been sprung, and there was no way out. I heard again Glenda's scream, and I shivered. I was not only dealing with a devil, but also a madman.

I drove back to Sharnville in despair.

At 08.30, I walked into the police station house.

This day was Friday: a hot, sticky morning with high humidity, but with clear sky and a bright sun.

I had spent a bad night, tossing and turning, with Glenda constantly on my mind. My face, where Benny had hit me, had been bruised, but Jebson's ointment had cleared the bruise during the night. I shrank from facing Klaus again, but I had to get the parcel from Maclain and deliver it.

Deputy sheriff Tim Bentley sat at his desk. He was a good cop, but young. He would have made a much better sheriff than Maclain. He was tall, rangy with fiery red hair and freckles. He grinned at me as I came in.

'Hi, Mr Lucas. Anything I can do?'

'Maclain in yet, Tim?'

'Had to go to LA last night, Mr Lucas. I don't expect him back until Monday.'

I stiffened.

'I gave him a parcel on Wednesday evening to be delivered to Mr Brannigan,' I said. 'He put it in the safe.'

Bentley nodded.

'Sure. I know about that. The Sheriff took it with him.'

I had sudden difficulty in breathing, and my sticky sweat turned cold.

'I've got to get that parcel back!' My voice was harsh, and seeing Bentley's startled expression, I fought to control my rising panic. 'The arrangement was, Tim, that Maclain should deliver the parcel on Monday, and not before.'

'Sure, Mr Lucas. He knows that, but as he had urgent business in LA last night, and planned to stay over the weekend, he took the parcel with him. It's okay. He'll deliver it on Monday.'

'The parcel, Tim, contains plans for a new bank. I've just found that a lot of the costing is wrong. I've got to get it back right now!'

'I'll call LA and find out where Maclain is.'

I kept thinking of Klaus' vicious, snarling face. If I didn't deliver the parcel to him by this morning, he would take it out on Glenda.

After talking, Bentley put down the telephone receiver.

'Captain Perrell saw Maclain last night, Mr Lucas, and concluded the business. He doesn't know where Maclain is right now.' Bentley shrugged. 'He could be returning here or having himself a weekend ball. You know what he's like.' He shrugged. 'He did tell me not to expect him back until Monday evening.'

I really flipped my lid. Crashing my fist down on the desk, I shouted, 'I've got to get that parcel back! I was out of my mind to have entrusted it to that drunken sod! You've got to help me, Tim!'

He regarded me with startled eyes.

'Hey, Mr Lucas! Take it easy. I ...'

'Do you mean you can't find him! What the hell are the police for? You've got to find him! If I let Brannigan see those figures, my firm will lose the contract! It's as important as that, and goddamn it, I'll hold Maclain and you responsible!'

'Well, if it's that important ...' He hesitated, then picked up the telephone receiver. He called LA again, and said it was urgent for them to find Maclain. He hung up.

'They'll find him, Mr Lucas, but it could take time. Suppose I call you at your office.'

'How long will it be?'

'Depends if Maclain is sober or not. I guess a couple of hours.'

'And if he's drunk?'

He shrugged.

'Your guess is as good as mine.'

'Call LA again. Tell them what I've told you. I'll drive out there right away. Let me use your phone.'

'Go ahead, Mr Lucas.'

I called my office, and told Mary I had to go to Los Angeles, but I would be back some time this afternoon.

'But, Mr Lucas, you have three appointments.'

'Cancel them,' I said, and hung up. 'I'm on my way, Tim. Thanks for what you're doing,' and I went back to my car.

By now it was 09.00. It would take me around two hours of fast driving to reach Los Angeles. There could be a delay getting the parcel. I didn't think I could get to Klaus before 15.00.

I walked fast to the post office, then realised I hadn't Klaus' telephone number. I looked him up in the book, but he was unlisted. Sweat was pouring off me. I dialled Directory Enquiries. I got a helpful operator.

'This is an emergency,' I said. 'I must contact Mr Edwin Klaus. He lives at The Farmhouse, Shannon Road. Please connect me.'

'Hold a moment, sir.' There was a delay, then she came back to me. 'I'm sorry, sir, this is an unlisted number.'

'I know that. His son has been badly injured in a car accident. I've got to alert his father. This is Doctor Lewis talking.'

A long hesitation.

'Okay, doctor, I'll connect you.'

I wiped the sweat off my face as I waited, then Benny's harsh voice came over the line.

'What is it?'

'Give me Klaus,' I half shouted. 'This is Lucas.'

'What makes you think he wants to talk to you, fink? Get stuffed!'

'Get him, you ape!' I yelled.

There was a pause, then I heard talking, then Klaus came on the line.

'Yes, Mr Lucas?'

'The police have taken the parcel to Los Angeles. I'm going there right now, but I can't get back to you before four o'clock.'

'At exactly four o'clock, Mr Lucas, unless you have arrived, Benny will be allowed free access to your woman,' and he hung up.

It wasn't until just after 11.00 that I reached the Los Angeles station house.

Captain Perrell, a short, heavily built man, knew I played golf with Brannigan, so I got the VIP treatment.

'I've got your problem solved for you, Mr Lucas,' he said. 'Although we haven't found Maclain, we found his deputy who is already on his way back to Sharnville. He tells me

Maclain is spending the weekend with some woman, but Maclain told him to deliver the parcel you're worried about to the bank. He did this at 09.30 this morning and got a receipt.' He handed me a slip of paper.

Received one parcel from Mr Lucas, Sharnville, for Mr Farrell Brannigan.
Lois Shelton.
Secretary to Mr Brannigan.

I knew Lois Shelton well.

'Thanks, Captain, I'll get over to the bank.'

As I returned to my car, I asked myself if Brannigan had already opened the parcel and had read my statement. Entering the bank, I asked to speak to Miss Shelton. The receptionist smiled at me.

'Go ahead, Mr Lucas. I guess, by now, you know your way up.'

I took the elevator to the top floor and walked into Lois Shelton's office.

She was tall, dark, slim and nice looking without being pretty.

'Why, Larry, what brings you here?' she asked, pushing back her desk chair.

'You signed for a parcel for FB,' I said. 'Has he got it?'

Sweat was running down my face, and my voice was a croak.

'Is anything wrong?' She looked alarmed as she got to her feet.

'Has he got it?'

'It's on his desk right now. He's away for the weekend. Is it something important?'

I sucked in a deep breath.

'He's away?'

'Yes ... he left last night. He said he was taking a golfing weekend.'

'I've just found out my calculator is on the blink. The figures in that parcel are all haywire. If FB sees them, he'll throw the book at me.'

She laughed.

'Don't look so worried. It happens. I'll get it for you.'

While I was waiting, an idea jumped into my mind. I had already made a copy of my statement and the tapes which Klaus now held. Why not make a third copy? I looked at my watch. It was just after 12.00. If I worked fast, I could still return to Sharnville by 16.00.

Lois came in with the parcel.

'Lois – a favour. Can you let me have the use of two tape recorders and a photocopy machine?'

'Of course. Come with me.'

She took me into a small office.

'There you are: two tape recorders and a photocopy machine. Anything else?'

'No ... fine. I won't be long.'

Hearing her desk telephone bell begin to ring, she gave me a little wave and left me.

It took me a little over an hour to copy the two tapes and take a copy of my statement. I also made a photocopy of the bonds. I repacked the parcel, then put the photocopies of my statement and the bonds and the duplicate tapes into a big envelope I found in a desk drawer, sealed the envelope and wrote on it:

To be delivered to Mr Brannigan on July 5th, and not before.

Today was June 29th. This would give me time to manoeuvre. If Klaus completely outwitted me and I was killed, Brannigan would still have enough evidence to go after him, but if I had luck, and I survived the break-in, I could get the parcel back from Lois.

I went into her office and put the envelope on her desk.

'I want you to give this to FB, Lois, on July 5th, and not before. It contains ideas for a new system of security. I'm still working on it. If you don't hear from me by July 4th, give it to him the following morning. I could have a change of mind, then I'll call you, and come over and collect it. It sounds a bit like James Bond, but it is important to me. Okay?'

Looking puzzled, Lois nodded.

'I'll lock it in my safe. No problem.'

'Thanks. I've got to get back to Sharnville,' and blowing her a kiss, I took the elevator down to the ground floor, holding onto the parcel, got into my car and headed back to Sharnville.

I drove up the dirt road leading to Klaus' house as the hands of my watch moved to 15.15.

Benny opened the front door as I walked up the steps.

'So you made it, fink,' he said. 'My bad luck. I was looking forward to giving your whore a workout.'

I walked into the living-room where Klaus was sitting at his desk and I put the parcel in front of him.

'Open it, Mr Lucas.'

I ripped off the string and brown paper, opened the briefcase and let him see the original statement, the two tapes and the forged bonds.

He nodded.

'You have done what you have been told to do. That is sensible, Mr Lucas.' He stared at me, and there was a look in those icy-green eyes that frightened me. After a long pause, he went on, 'Now if I had been an amateur as you are an amateur, before parting with the contents of this briefcase, I would have made two further copies of the tapes and have photocopied the statement and the bonds ... if I had been an amateur like you, Mr Lucas. I would have left them with the bank with instructions to give them to Mr Brannigan on his return from his golfing weekend. Did you do that, Mr Lucas?'

He's a devil! I heard Glenda's despairing voice.

Somehow, I kept my face expressionless. Somehow I forced my eyes to meet his probing glare.

'I wish to God I had thought of that,' I said, huskily.

His smile sent a chill through me.

'I propose to call Miss Shelton, and you will ask her if the package you left with her is safe.'

Benny came into the room, and stood against the wall, grinning.

'I have an extension, Mr Lucas, so I will hear what she says.'

He began to dial.

He is a devil!

My bluff called, and feeling utterly defeated, I said, 'She has copies.'

He replaced the receiver and stared at me with that maniacal glare, then he looked at Benny.

'I leave this stupid amateur to you. Try not to make too much of a mess,' and getting to his feet, he walked by me, and out of the room.

Grinning evilly, Benny moved away from the wall.

'Fink, this is going to be a pleasure,' he said. 'When a fink gets beaten by me, he knows he's been beaten.'

Moving swiftly, he brushed my jaw with his left, and then, as I threw up my hands, he slammed a right that felt like a chunk of concrete into my stomach.

Slowly, I drifted back to consciousness. Far away, as if in a dream, I heard Glenda's voice saying, 'Oh, my darling, what have they done to you?'

I moved, and pain like the snapping of a wolf's teeth gripped me so violently I cried out.

'Don't move.'

My eyelids felt leaden, but I forced them up. Dimly, and out of focus, I saw Glenda's red hair, then her face.

'Don't say anything. Wait, Larry. Don't move. Just wait.'

My eyelids were too heavy to support, and I drifted away into unconsciousness.

The next time I became aware of her, her face was in focus: a white, drawn face, but Glenda's face, and it was close to mine. I felt her lips brush against my cheek. I groped for her hand and held it.

'Don't try to move, darling,' she said. 'It'll wear off ... be patient.'

'What have they been doing to you?' I managed to ask.

Her hand tightened on mine.

'Never mind about me. Please listen, Larry. You must get them into the bank. I told you he is a devil. You wouldn't listen. Oh, darling, why did you have to act smart? Look at what they have done to you. If you only knew what they have done to me.'

I lay still, riding the pain of my bruised body. I felt as if something had broken inside me. I thought of Alex Marsh who had sat crying while they had beaten Glenda. He had lost his guts. The scientific beating Benny had given me had reduced me to utter terror that he would do it again, and yet deep in my subconscious, there began to grow a burning desire to kill him, to kill Klaus, to kill Harry and to kill Joe. But I knew this desire to kill them was way out of reach, but it was there, and growing.

'Don't worry. I'll get them in.'

'Oh, darling! I can't stand being locked up here with that thug any longer.'

I then became aware I was lying on a bed, and looking around, I saw we were in a small room with the window boarded up. Opposite, was a half-open door, leading to a bathroom.

'Is this where they keep you?'

'Yes. Benny brought you in here and told me to take care of you. I think Klaus and he have gone somewhere.'

'You mean we are alone?'

'I think so.'

I made a tremendous effort and sat up. My body raged with pain. She tried to stop me, but I pushed her hands away.

'This is our chance! We've got to break out!' Sweat broke out on my face as I swung my feet to the floor. 'Help me up, Glenda.'

'You can't get out! Don't you think I've tried and tried?'

'Help me up!'

Supporting me, as I dragged myself upright, she said, 'It's no good, Larry. You'll only hurt yourself.'

I staggered over to the door and put my hands on the panel. The door was as solid as a brick wall. Even with an axe, I would have had trouble to break it down. Turning to the window, I found the boards were of oak, screwed in. There was no hope of getting out through the door nor the window.

The pain raging through me made me feel faint, and I slumped down on the bed.

Glenda ran into the bathroom and returned with a glass of water. I poured the water over my head, and the dizziness went away. As I handed her the glass, I looked at my watch. For a moment, I couldn't believe it. I had been unconscious for more than four hours.

'We might break through the ceiling,' I said.

'It's too high. There's nothing to stand on. Nothing to use! Oh, Larry, darling, we must do what he tells us!'

Then we heard a sound outside, and Glenda clutched hold of me. A moment later, the door jerked open, and Klaus walked in.

Behind him, pausing in the open doorway, were Benny and Joe.

'By now, Mr Lucas, you will realise it is most unwise to play tricks with me.' Klaus turned to Glenda. 'A glass of water.'

Picking up the glass, she almost ran into the bathroom. It sickened me to see how terrified she was of him.

'Here are some pills, Mr Lucas. Take them! I want you to be fit and ready for the operation.'

Benny, followed by Joe, lounged into the room.

There was nothing I could do. The thought of Benny's massive fists smashing into my aching body made me cringe. I took the three pills, then the glass of water which Glenda put shakily into my hand.

'Take them!' Klaus snarled.

I swallowed the pills and drank the water.

'I'm sure you won't object to sharing your woman's bed,' Klaus said, 'Good night to you both,' and he left the room.

'I'll be right outside, fink, if you want anything during the night,' Benny said. He lifted his great fists. 'You have only to ask.'

Joe let out a bellow of laughter, then they backed out of the room, and I heard the bolt slam shut.

As I reached for Glenda's hand, the pills hit me and I went out like an extinguished light.

7

I dreamed Joe was playing the spiritual on his harmonica. I moved, hoping to break the dream, then I abruptly came awake, and still the tune persisted.

I opened my eyes, and there was Joe, sitting on a stool, playing his harmonica, and seeing me staring at him, he stopped playing, and his thick lips moved into a wide grin.

'Hi, there, man,' he said. 'Time to get up.'

I sat up on the bed. There was no agonising pain, but my body ached. I looked around.

Seated on the floor, in a corner, was Glenda. She looked at me, her big eyes dull.

'Come on, man,' Joe said. 'Have a bath. I'll fix it for you. Time's getting on. You can't sleep forever.'

I looked at my watch. The time was ten o'clock. I had no idea if it was ten in the morning or night.

Joe opened the door and called. A moment later, Benny came in. He went over to Glenda, grabbed her arm and hauled her to her feet.

'Nice walk now, baby,' he said, and hustled her out of the room.

Joe went into the bathroom and turned on the bath taps.

I got to my feet, expecting sharp pains, but there were no pains. This was something I wasn't going to let Joe know about. As he came out of the bathroom, I drew in a shuddering breath, and bent double.

'Come on, come on, man,' he said impatiently. 'You ain't that soft.'

I remained still, bent double, then hobbled slowly to the bathroom. I stood by the bath, breathing heavily as Joe turned off the taps. He pulled off my shirt.

'Yeah, man. Benny certainly can do a job.'

I looked down at my chest. It was yellow, black and blue. Taking my time, making out I was much more feeble than I was, I got out of my trousers and pants, then naked, I reeled back, thudding against Joe who grabbed me.

'Come on, man!' he said impatiently, and half shoved, half lifted me into the bath.

I lay in the hot water, my eyes closed, but my mind now active. There must be some way out of this trap! As long as Glenda was a hostage, I was powerless. If I could only find some way to free her ...

Joe stood over me, and let me soak in the hot water for some ten minutes, then he reached down, grabbed my wrist and hauled me upright. I released a groan for his benefit.

'Dry yourself, and hurry it up, man. The boss wants you,' and he went into the bedroom.

I took my time. Touching my bruised body was bad, but I dried myself, slowly put on my shirt, climbed into my trousers and moved slowly into the bedroom. I was surprised that my movements gave me no pain, but I was careful to groan at every step.

'Want something to eat, man?' Joe asked, and waved to a tray containing a jug of coffee and sandwiches.

I realised I was ravenously hungry. Careful to move slowly, I poured coffee and sipped.

'What time is it, Joe?'

135

'Night time,' he said. 'Those pills the boss gave you sure knocked you out.'

I was feeling stronger now. The coffee helped. I ate the sandwiches, standing and half bent over, while Joe sat on the stool, playing his harmonica. I felt even better when I had finished the meal.

'You know something, man?' Joe said, putting the harmonica in his shirt pocket. 'You sure brought trouble on yourself. I told you the boss was smart, and you wouldn't listen. I told you, not to dig your own grave. Still, you wouldn't listen. I told you, working for the boss, you would get on the gravy train, like me, but you wouldn't listen. So you had to do it the hard way.'

I straightened slightly and looked at him.

'I'm still warning you, Joe,' I said. 'A black boy means nothing to Klaus. You are going to be taken for a ride like me.'

He grinned.

'That's what you say. Come on. The boss wants you.'

As he caught hold of my arm and moved me to the door, the door swung open and Benny shoved Glenda past me. The shove was so violent she went sprawling, landing on hands and knees.

I started towards her, but Benny blocked me off, shoving his fist into my face. I had an urge to hit him, but this wasn't the time. I let Joe lead me down the passage, and into the living-room.

Klaus was sitting at his desk.

Joe shoved me into a chair, facing Klaus, then stood back.

'All right, Joe,' Klaus said. 'Wait outside.'

Joe left the room, closing the door behind him.

'How do you feel, Mr Lucas?' Klaus asked, leaning forward and staring at me.

I sat, bent forward, my arms wrapped around my body.

'Mr Lucas!' There was a snap in his voice. 'Don't put on an act for me! You asked for a beating, and you got it. Be careful, you don't get another. In another four hours, you will lead my men into the bank. Is that understood?'

I lifted my head and stared at him.

'Yes.'

'There are things to do. Now once again, Mr Lucas, I warn you: no more tricks if you want your woman to stay alive. Understand?'

'Yes.'

'Very well. Now in case you are wondering if you will be reported missing by your secretary, I can tell you she has received a telegram saying you have been delayed, and she can expect you on Tuesday. That will give you plenty of time to go on the run.'

I was sure once the three had stripped out the bank, they would murder me. I had no illusions about that.

I didn't say anything.

He pressed a bell button, and Harry came in.

'Take care of him, Harry, and watch him.'

Harry grinned at me: cocky, confident and sexy.

'Let's go buster,' he said. 'You've had your try, now, it's strictly business.'

I got slowly to my feet, and still hunched forward, I followed him out of the room and into the hot, steamy night.

Harry switched on a powerful flashlight and walked with me across the lawn to a big barn. We entered.

The barn was lit by two naked bulbs, hanging from the rafters. In the middle of the barn stood a security truck. It was a facsimile of the truck I had seen so often on Sharnville's Main Street. Standing by it were two tall, thick-set men, wearing the brown uniforms of the Security Company.

'Take a look, buster,' Harry said. 'What do you think?'

The two men eyed me as I looked them over, then I walked slowly around the truck. I couldn't fault either the uniforms or the truck.

'It's a good job,' I said.

Harry nodded and grinned.

'I guess. Make sure, buster. Take another look. We don't want to slip up, do we?'

'It's a good job,' I repeated.

'Watch this.'

He opened the driver's door, leaned in and pulled a lever. The Security Company's name, printed in red letters on either side of the truck, slid out of sight into the roof of the truck: another panel appeared with the lettering: Calo Furniture Co. The licence plate swivelled over to a Los Angeles number.

'Cute, huh?' Harry said. 'We all take off in the truck, once it's loaded.'

All except me, I thought.

'Pretty neat,' I said.

'Okay. Now we'll go to your pad and collect your gimmicks. Let's go.'

We left the barn and crossed the lawn to where the Chevvy was parked.

'You drive, buster. I'll watch you.'

With him sitting by my side, I started the engine and drove onto the dirt road.

Harry said, 'I've been thinking about you, buster, and what you said to me. Where you went wrong was to trust Joe. Now Joe is a simple black boy. The boss has taken care of him, and when a simple black boy believes in someone, he stays with him. Everything you said to Joe went back to the boss. It was the boss' idea for Joe to give you a gun. The boss is smart. He looks ahead all the time. He figured unless

Joe gave you a gun, you would buy one for yourself. That's looking ahead. It was a fine idea of yours to get Joe to get Glenda out. The idea was fine, but you went wrong in thinking you could trust Joe. So what happens? You get a beating, and Glenda is still locked up.'

I didn't say anything. I slowed at the end of the dirt road, and waited for a break in the traffic before moving on to the highway.

'I'm not kidding myself,' Harry went on, 'that there's three million in the vault. I think Klaus is as nutty as you say he is. Maybe there's a million. A million split up by three isn't so hot. Here's a proposition, buster. You have Glenda and fifty thousand bucks, and I have the rest. Like the idea?'

Was this yet another con? I asked myself.

'What would happen to Joe and Benny?'

'Tell me something. If a gun went off in the vault could it be heard on the street?'

'It wouldn't even be heard in the bank.'

'I was wondering about that. The idea I've got is when the cartons are packed, I knock off Joe and Benny, then I give you fifty grand and a gun. I take off in the truck with the rest of the loot, and you go out and knock off Klaus, and get Glenda. This car will be parked near the bank. You use it. How about it?'

And what is there to stop you shooting me after you have shot Joe and Benny? I thought.

'How about the two men handling the truck?'

'No problem. As soon as they drive into the cellar, they leave. They have their own getaway car. It is after the loot is in the truck that I go into action. I'll be handling the money. I'll put fifty grand in one of the cartons. As soon as

139

I've knocked off Joe and Benny, I give you the carton and a gun, and you're on your own, and I'm on my own.'

We were now driving down Sharnville's main street. I turned off and headed for my apartment block.

'Klaus will be on his own with Glenda?'

'Sure. There's no one else. All you have to do is walk in and knock him off. Like the idea?'

If I lived to reach Klaus after the break-in, I liked it, but I trusted Harry the way I would trust a rattlesnake. It would be too easy for him. Bang – and Benny was dead. Bang – and Joe was dead, and bang again – I was dead.

'Yes,' I said. 'I like it.'

He leaned forward and patted my knee.

'Okay, buster. It's a deal.'

I parked outside my apartment block, then shifted around in the driving seat so I could look at Harry. The light from the street lamp fell directly on his face.

'Tell me something, Harry,' I said. 'Doesn't it mean a thing to you to kill Joe and Benny? You could just shoot them down, and it would mean nothing to you?'

He grinned.

'Let me put it this way, buster: to get Glenda, would you give a damn about putting a bullet in Klaus?'

For a long moment, I thought about this. If I didn't kill Klaus, he would certainly kill Glenda and me. I was sure of that.

'I guess you have a point,' I said.

'To get a million bucks, why should I care if I knock off a couple of stumblebums like Joe and Benny? Who would miss them anyway?'

I opened the car and got out on to the sidewalk. Harry joined me, and we rode up the elevator to my apartment.

While Harry lounged around, I quickly put together the gimmicks I needed to get into the bank. I found a plastic sack in the kitchen and put the gimmicks in it.

I looked at my watch. The time was now 01.10. Time was running out.

'All fixed,' I said, putting the sack on the table.

'Got everything?'

'Yes.'

'Sure? We don't want a foul-up because you've forgotten something.'

'All fixed.'

'Okay.' He moved to a chair and sat down. 'How about a drink?'

I went to my liquor cabinet and took out a bottle of Scotch and two glasses. I made two mild drinks, gave him one, and then went over and sat near him. He lifted his glass.

'Here's to success. Now, listen, here's what we do.' He drank, put down his glass and leaned forward. 'Klaus has told me to stay close to you. He doesn't trust you, but don't worry about that. You and me will go up to Manson's office while Joe and Benny remain by the vault door. You do your telephone and cassette act. You open the vault and Joe gets to work. He really knows his stuff with a cutter. You say there are four hundred boxes to open. Benny and me will take the loot from the boxes as Joe opens them, and we'll pack the money in the cartons. You just keep out of the way. If Joe works fast, maybe I'll get you to help fill the cartons. We work all through Saturday. We have around twenty-seven hours to bust into all the boxes. The truck arrives at eight o'clock, Sunday morning, and the driver and his pal take off. We load the cartons into the truck.' Harry paused, and grinned. 'While Benny and Joe are clearing up,

I knock them off. I give you a gun and a carton with fifty grand in it, and you go after Klaus. Got it?'

I drank some of my whisky.

Would Harry shoot me as soon as I got them into the vault? My mind worked swiftly. I thought that unlikely. None of them would want a dead body with them in the vault for twenty-seven hours. No … when Harry had shot Joe and Benny, I would be next.

'I've got it,' I said.

'Joe handles the cutter. Benny handles the cartons. You'll handle your gimmicks and a sack of food. I've got that packed and ready. No point in starving. My chick will be ready to chat up the guard.' He looked at his watch. 'Another hour and a half.'

He got to his feet and began to roam around my room.

'All that money!' he exclaimed. 'This is something I've dreamed about!'

'Those bonds Klaus gave me,' I said, watching him. 'Joe tells your father did them. They looked good to me.'

He paused and grinned at me.

'Joe talks too much.' He laughed, cocky and confident. 'Yes, Klaus made you a sucker. Those bonds would look good to anyone. My father was an artist, but he was also stupid. He was so goddamn greedy, he got careless and he landed himself and me in jail. Working together, we could have made a fortune, but he tried to rush it, and a set of bonds were spotted. We had the Feds after us.' He shrugged. 'That's the way the cookie crumbles, but this time, I'm not handling dud bonds, I'm handling real money.'

'And what are you going to do when you get the money, Harry?'

'A million – maybe more! With that kind of bread, a smart guy like me can drop out of sight.' He gave me a sly grin. 'With that kind of bread, I can buy me a regiment of women. That's my thing – women. I'll keep moving and keep screwing. I can't wait to start.'

'Once the police are alerted, Harry, they'll come after you.'

He laughed.

'They've come after me before. I'll get lost this time. They only caught up with me last time because I had no money, but with a million – I've got no problems.' He scratched at his beard. 'What do you plan to do with fifty grand and Glenda?'

This was something I hadn't thought about. Just suppose Harry wasn't conning me, and he did give me fifty thousand dollars and a gun, and I did get Glenda ... what would I do?

I knew the moment the police found I had left Sharnville, they would come after me, knowing that I was behind the bank break-in. But the bank break-in wouldn't be discovered until 08.30 Monday morning. If Harry wasn't conning me, I would have twenty-four hours to get out of the country.

'I guess I'll fly to Canada,' I said. 'Once there, I'll have time to make plans.'

He nodded, and again his grin was sly.

'Glenda's a smart cookie. You two talk it over. She'll fix something.'

I looked at my watch. I had another hour to wait.

'I'm still feeling pretty bad, Harry. While we wait, I'll rest on my bed. Okay with you?'

'Go ahead.' He poured himself another drink. 'Waiting around is hell.'

I went into my bedroom and stretched out on the bed. I was sure Harry wouldn't give me fifty thousand dollars, and I was even more sure he wouldn't give me a gun. I lay still and thought. I concentrated my thoughts on the vault. Harry, Joe, Benny and I would be in the vault for some twenty-seven hours. I thought of the slide-up door in the vault that gave access to the cellar garage. I had so arranged this door that when it opened, the vault doors automatically closed. The electronic control which opened the slide-up door was operated by a press button, inserted in the wall by the slide-up door, and painted white, as the walls were painted white. The button was practically invisible unless you knew where to look for it.

I continued to think, and finally, a risky solution to my problem began to take shape.

I was still lying on the bed, still thinking, when Harry looked in.

'Time to move, buster,' he said. 'Let's go.'

I got off the bed, put on my jacket and went into the living-room. The time was now 02.35. I picked up the plastic sack containing my gimmicks and tools.

'You're sure you've forgotten nothing?' Harry asked.

'I'm sure.'

'You feeling okay?'

'I'll survive.'

'Benny's watching the bank. When the guard goes around the back of the bank, Benny's going to light a cigarette. I've got my chick staked out, waiting to chat up the guard. As soon as Benny lights a cigarette, we move in fast.'

We got in the elevator and rode down to the ground floor. I wondered, as I moved out of the elevator, if I had many more hours in which to live.

We went on to the street.

Car headlights flashed, then died.

'That's Joe,' Harry said.

The Chevvy was parked a few yards down the street. We reached it, then I saw Harry stiffen and stop short.

I could see Joe sitting at the driving wheel. There was another man, sitting in the back of the car.

'Come along, Harry. Time is running out.'

With a cold sense of shock, I recognised Klaus' clipped voice.

Klaus!

I heard Harry say, his voice uncertain, 'You here, boss?'

'I have decided to join in the fun,' Klaus said. 'You sit in front, Harry. Mr Lucas will sit beside me.'

As I got into the car and sat beside Klaus, I saw he was holding a revolver which pointed at me.

As Harry dropped into the front passenger's seat, Joe engaged gear and drove the car at a sedate pace towards the National Californian Bank.

As we drove through the deserted streets and swung into Main Street, my mind was working furiously.

Here was Klaus, seated by my side! What had happened to Glenda? Had he already murdered her? My insides cringed at the thought. If not, would he have left her unguarded?

Klaus said quietly, 'I can read your thoughts, Mr Lucas. Your woman is quite safe. I have arranged for a guard to look after her. When you have done your job, there will be no problem. You and she will be free to do what you wish.'

A psychopath!

If he imagined I believed one word he was saying, he was crazier than I believed he was!

Joe swung the car to the kerb and dowsed the lights. We were within two hundred yards of the bank.

From where I sat, I could see the bank's guard, sitting in his sentry-box. I knew him, having once played golf with him: an ex-cop with a nice wife and four children.

Joe kept the engine running while we all sat watching the guard. The hands of the dashboard clock moved to 03.11.

'Get moving, you sonofabitch,' Harry muttered.

We waited another ten minutes, then the guard yawned, stretched himself, and stepped out of his sentry-box. He looked to right and left, then with his rifle slung on his shoulder, he began to plod slowly along the front of the bank.

Joe shifted into gear and moved the car forward.

'Take it easy,' Harry said. 'Wait for Benny.'

Joe stopped the car.

Harry turned around to look at me.

'You take the food sack and your gimmicks. Are you ready to open the bank doors?'

'Yes,' I said, and accepted the plastic sack he shoved over the seat at me.

We waited. The guard was now out of sight. Then across the way, in a dark doorway, a match flared up. Joe moved the car fast to within ten yards of the bank's entrance and parked.

'Get the doors open!' Klaus snapped at me.

I slid out of the car, as Joe ran around to open the trunk. Benny joined us and grabbed a pile of collapsible cartons that Joe handed to him. I used the neutraliser and the bank doors slid open.

Klaus was first to enter, and he paused, facing the rest of us as we rushed in.

'Stay right here.' He looked at me. 'Are we safe here from the alarm beam?'

'It's six feet behind you,' I said, and using the neutraliser, I closed the bank doors.

The whole operation had taken less than forty seconds.

'Well, we're in,' Benny said, grinning.

'You and Harry open the vault,' Klaus said to me, regarding me with his ice-grey eyes. 'No tricks, Mr Lucas, or you won't leave here alive. We'll wait here.'

I dropped on hands and knees and crawled under the invisible beam, then I stood up. Following my movements, Harry joined me. Again using the neutraliser, I opened the elevator doors.

'This will take a little time,' I said to Klaus.

Klaus glared at Harry, 'Watch him!'

I pressed the second floor button and the elevator doors swished closed, and the cage started its smooth journey upwards.

'Jeeze!' Harry exploded. 'Who the hell would expect him to show up!'

The elevator doors opened. Using my flashlight, I walked fast to Manson's office. I pushed open the door, and followed by Harry, I entered.

Keeping the beam of my flashlight away from the windows, I sat at Manson's desk and reached for the red telephone. I knew exactly what I had to do so I didn't have to think about it. My mind was busy with this unexpected arrival of Klaus.

As I began to cut and strip the telephone leads, Harry said, 'If you and me don't work together, buster, you won't get Glenda, and I won't get the bread.'

Without pausing in what I was doing, I asked, 'Has he got someone to guard Glenda?'

'Not a chance. Why should he? Who's he got? She's locked in, and she can't get out. Don't worry about her. Here's what we do: I take care of Joe and Benny, and you take care of Klaus.'

I began to splice the wires of my gimmick to the cut wires of the telephone.

147

'Take care of him? How?'

'You any good with a gun?'

I paused and stared at him.

'I've never handled a gun.'

He grimaced.

'Klaus is good. You've got to get real close to him. If you get close enough, you can't miss.' He laid a flat automatic pistol on the desk in front of me. 'We wait until the truck arrives tomorrow morning. Then while Joe and Benny are loading the loot into the truck, get close to Klaus and give it to him. Shoot through your jacket pocket. The moment you shoot, I'll take Joe and Benny. That's no problem. They'll be handling the cartons. Okay?'

'How do I know Klaus hasn't already murdered Glenda?'

'And land himself with her body? He plays smart. If he's going to knock her off, he'll get Benny to bury her. You don't have to worry about her. She's okay right now. You knock Klaus off, and all you have to do is to drive out there, pick her up, and be on your way.'

I didn't believe a word he was saying, but I knew I had to go along with him for the time being. At least, now I had a gun.

I finished the telephone wiring. As I reached for the gun, I said, 'Is it loaded?'

'Sure.' Harry took the gun from my hand, removed the clip and showed me the bullets. He replaced the clip. 'All you have to do is to thumb back this catch, and point the gun through your jacket pocket at Klaus' guts and squeeze the trigger. Don't pull or jerk the trigger ... squeeze it.'

Knowing this was something I could never bring myself to do, I took the gun from him and dropped it into my pocket.

'Have you got this fixed?' Harry asked, and waved to the telephone.

'It's ready to go.' Using the dial, I dialled 2-4-6-8. I waited, then heard clicking sounds. 'That's it! Three of the locks are now unlocked.'

'Jeeze!' He stared at the telephone. 'It's goddamn magic.'

Leaving the desk, I went to the wall behind Manson's chair. I found the sliding panel and took out the tape cassette. Locating another hidden panel, I thumbed it open and fed the cassette into the slot. After a wait of some fifteen seconds a green light showed.

'The vault's open now.' I moved back to the desk and stripped out the gimmick and dropped it into the plastic sack.

Watching me, Harry said, 'You really mean the vault's open?'

I dropped the wire cutter into my pocket as I said, 'It's open.'

'Once you know how, huh?' He gave an uneasy grin. His face shone with sweat and his eyes were uneasy. 'Watch Klaus. He's real fast with a gun. For Pete's sake, don't miss him.'

My heart thumping, I rode down with him in the elevator.

The vault doors stood open. Klaus, Joe and Benny were already in the vault.

As Harry and I walked in, Klaus turned.

'So far, Mr Lucas, you have succeeded,' he said. 'Now if you will stand over there, and keep out of the way, the operation can proceed.' He waved me to the far wall as Joe began to assemble his cutter, and Benny busied himself with the cartons.

Harry looked around the vault, lined with safe deposit boxes.

'Some joint,' he said.

'Yes, Harry. Each of those little boxes leads to money,' Klaus said.

I moved away and leaned my back against the far wall, close to the steel shutter that guarded the entrance to the cellar garage. Moving slightly to my right, my body concealed the control button that would open the shutter, and at the same time, shut the vault doors.

By now, Joe had the flame of the cutter alight.

'Where do I start, boss?' he asked.

Klaus pointed to the first box on the right wall.

'Be careful, Joe. Just take the lock out.'

Joe adjusted his goggles, then turned up the flame. Klaus and the other two watched him. I moved my hand behind me and felt the control button. My fingers moved over it. This wasn't the time, I told myself, and I felt sweat running down my spine.

It took Joe ten minutes before he cut out the lock, and as the lock dropped to the floor, he lowered the flame and stepped back.

'That door's hot,' he said.

Harry came forward. He was now wearing an asbestos glove on his right hand. He jerked open the door of the box, then let out a curse.

'Nothing!'

'Keep going, Joe,' Klaus said. 'Try to make it faster. There are four hundred boxes to open. You've taken ten minutes to open one. At this rate, it'll take you sixty hours and more to open the lot.'

Joe gaped at him.

'You said to be careful, boss.'

'Don't be all that careful!' Klaus snapped.

Joe had the next lock out in a little over five minutes. Again Harry moved forward and jerked open the door.

'Hey!'

Benny came forward. The two men peered into the box.

150

'Boy! Look! Money!' Benny exclaimed.

'Clear it, and get on!' Klaus snapped.

While Harry was clearing the contents of the box, Joe began on the third box. This time, he got the lock cut out in four minutes. Without waiting for Harry to open the box, he moved to the fourth box.

'Money!' Harry exclaimed, and began to shovel neatly packaged dollar bills into the carton Benny was holding.

I was watching Klaus. His thin face was tense. His eyes were riveted on Joe as Joe cut into the fourth box. There was an impatient expectancy about Klaus, like a man waiting anxiously for the result of vitally important news: the result of a diagnosis that could prove fatal.

At all our meetings, Klaus had been cold and calm, but not now. As the fourth lock burned out, and Harry jerked open the door of the box, Klaus moved forward. From the box, Harry pulled out three leather jewel cases and a stack of money. Klaus peered into the box, then muttering, he stepped back.

I felt suddenly sure that he hadn't, as he had said, 'come to join in the fun'. He was here to get something from one of these boxes: something that meant much to him.

Joe was working faster now. He cut out the fifth lock in under three minutes.

'Be careful!' Klaus snarled at him.

Harry opened the door of the box, then grunted.

'Papers,' he said in disgust.

Klaus pushed him aside, and pulled out various documents. He examined them quickly, then threw them on the floor. Then I knew for certain he was looking for some special document.

The sixth box yielded a pile of money and several documents. While Klaus was examining the documents, and Harry and Benny were putting the money into a carton, and Joe was busy cutting into the seventh lock, I pressed the control button, leaning my back hard against the shutter.

It happened in split seconds.

The vault door slammed shut. The shutter snapped up, and I fell into the garage.

I had a brief sight of Klaus, Harry, Joe and Benny, turning to stare at the closed door of the vault. I scrambled to my feet, groped for the control button, my side of the wall. I found and pressed it, and as the shutter slammed shut, I saw Klaus, gun in hand, spin around, but he was just too late.

With my heart hammering, I pulled out my flashlight, snapped it on, and ran to the fuse box. I knew the right wire to cut. With a shaking hand, I inserted the wire cutter and cut the wire adrift.

Even if they found the control button inside the vault, the shutter would no longer work.

I had them trapped!

As I stood by the half-open garage door, looking cautiously out on to the side street, I glanced at my watch. The time now was 04.30. My thoughts were on Glenda.

The easiest and quickest thing to do was to take the Chevvy, parked outside the bank, but I decided against this. I had seen Joe remove the ignition key. The car was parked within ten yards of the sentry-box. I could have started the car, but it would have taken time, and have attracted the guard's attention.

I must get back to my apartment, and use my car. I peered up and down the deserted, narrow street, then closing the garage door, I began to run down the street, away from Main Street, turning left, running down another street, then turning left again, and I was on Main Street, but some hundred yards from the bank entrance. I then slowed to a fast walk.

Sharnville was asleep.

It took me twenty minutes, half running, half walking, to reach my apartment. During the journey, my mind was active. Although I was desperately anxious to get to Glenda, I had to provide for going on the run. I would need clothes. I had only three thousand dollars now, but that would be enough to get us both to Canada. I was confident, once there, I could find some means of earning more money.

Letting myself into my apartment, I paused to look around.

I had lived here now for more than four years. I felt a pang about leaving it. As I stood there, the realisation that I was now a fugitive, to be constantly hunted, hit me.

Going into my bedroom, I got out a big suitcase and packed most of my more useful clothes. I then returned to the living-room and collected my various work tools, calculators and tables of reference. Without them, I would be lost.

I had few valuable possessions. I took gold cuff-links, a heavy gold signet ring that I never wore, and which my father had given me, a silver cigarette box I had won in a golf tournament, and I was ready to go.

I paused once more to look around, then snapped off the lights and rode down in the elevator to the garage. I heaved the heavy suitcase into the trunk of the car, started the engine and drove up the ramp.

As I drove along the deserted Main Street, heading for the highway, I slowed as I passed the bank.

The guard, yawning, was in his sentry-box.

I wondered what the four men, trapped in the vault, were doing. There was no possible way for them to break out until Monday morning when Manson arrived.

They were desperate men. I had to warn Manson. If he opened the vault doors, even knowing that the vault had been tampered with, these four would come out, shooting. I had no illusions about that. I decided, when I reached the nearest Canadian airport from the border, I would telephone Manson and warn him so the bank could be surrounded by armed police.

Now, my thoughts switched to Glenda. I longed to see her face when I shot back the bolt and walked into her prison. We would drive immediately to the airport and take the first available plane to Canada.

I was now on the highway, which at this hour, was deserted, but I knew there were police patrols, so I was careful not to speed. It took me twenty minutes of careful driving to reach the dirt road leading to Klaus' place.

My heart now thumping, my thoughts of walking into that house and freeing Glenda churning in my mind, I pulled up before the closed gate.

As a precaution, I had turned off my headlights as I drove up the dirt road.

Klaus had said Glenda was guarded. In spite of what Harry had said, I was taking no chances.

As I got out of the car, I pulled the gun from my pocket. I stood by the gate and looked towards the house. It was in total darkness.

Was someone there, lurking behind the closed curtains, aware that I had arrived?

Gently, I opened the gate, far enough for me to slip through. The faint dawn light made me visible if anyone was watching from the house. I hesitated, then bracing myself, I ran quickly across the coarse grass of the lawn until I reached the front door.

I paused, then turned the door handle and gently pushed. The door opened. I looked into darkness, waited, listened, then hearing nothing, I stepped into the lobby. Again I paused, listening. Then slowly, the gun pointed ahead of me, my finger on the trigger, I began to move down the passage that led to Glenda's prison. Pausing again, I took out my flashlight.

If someone was lurking in the living-room, and came out shooting, I was as good as dead. The urge to see Glenda again was too much for me. I switched on the flashlight and swung its beam on the door ahead of me.

The door stood open!

Forgetting any danger of a possible ambush, I walked quickly into the room, groped for the light switch and snapped it on.

The bright light blinded me for a moment, then I took in the familiar room which Glenda and I had shared.

It came as a crushing blow when I saw Glenda wasn't there. I rushed into the bathroom ... no Glenda.

Not caring now, I snapped on the passage light, ran into the living-room and turned on the lights.

It took me only a few seconds to go over the whole house. No Glenda!

So Glenda

8

Faint sunlight came through the curtains and lit up the carpet. A blackbird shrilled a warning. The refrigerator in the kitchen started up with a growl.

I stirred and looked at my watch. The time was now 05.45. I had been sitting in a despairing heap in the living-room, crushed with the knowledge that I had been too late to save Glenda.

I was sure now that when I left with Harry, Benny had murdered her, and had buried her. My suspicions that Klaus would order her killing were now confirmed.

I thought of her, the only woman I had found that really meant something to me. I saw her again: her red hair, her eyes, and that lovely body.

Somewhere on this farm, she had been buried. I had to find her grave! I couldn't continue to sit here, grieving for her. Getting to my feet, I walked out into the cool early morning air. The sun, now rising above the trees, cast pale shadows.

I looked around. The barn? I crossed the lawn and entered the barn, then came to an abrupt standstill.

I had forgotten the faked security truck. There it was standing in the middle of the barn. I crossed to it, and looked through the driver's window. Lying on the bench seat were the two guards' uniforms. I checked my watch. In twenty-four hours, if not less, the two men, posing as guards, would be arriving. Here was danger! If they drove the truck down to the bank as arranged, and found they couldn't get into the cellar garage, what would they do? If the bank guard spotted them, trying to get in, would he set off an alarm?

My mind was in a turmoil, but the urgent need to find Glenda's grave prevailed. I looked around the barn, examining the hard, dirt floor. She certainly wasn't buried here. As I started to the door, I heard a car approaching.

My heart thumping, my hand in my pocket, gripping the butt of the gun, I moved out into the pale sunshine.

A shabby Chrysler car had pulled up close to where I had parked my car, and two men got out. I recognised them as the two men who were to act as guards.

Seeing me, they stopped short. They looked at each other as I waved to them. They had seen me with Harry, and I hoped they would imagine I was one of the gang.

As they came forward, I went to meet them.

The taller of the two peered suspiciously at me.

'Is it okay?' he asked. With a feeling of relief, I was sure they thought I was working for Klaus.

'The operation is off,' I said, my finger on the gun's trigger. 'The boss told me to come out here, and tell you. You can forget it.'

The man looked at his partner.

'You mean we don't handle the truck?'

'That's it. The operation is off.'

The shorter of the two demanded aggressively, 'How about the money?'

'You keep it. There's no problem.'

For a long moment they stared at me, then looking at each other, they grinned.

157

'Boy! That's good news! You tell the boss any time he wants us, we're ready ... okay?'

'I'll tell him.'

I watched them return to their car and drive away.

I spent the next hour, tramping around the farm. I found no newly dug ground. Defeated and crushed, I returned to the living-room of the house. The time now was 07.00.

I dropped into a chair. For some minutes, I submitted to my grief. Glenda was dead! I mourned for her for more than half an hour, recalling those precious moments we had spent together, then I began to accept the inevitable. Now, I asked myself, what was I going to do?

Going on the run with Glenda would have been an exciting challenge to me, but going on the run on my own was a frightening, lonely thought.

Forcing myself not to think of her, I began to consider my own position. Klaus and his three men were trapped in the vault. There was no escape for them, but there was also little chance of escape for me. Once the police swung into action, they would know I was the only possible suspect who could have broken into the safest bank in the world.

Suddenly I didn't care any more. Being a fugitive, being hunted day and night without Glenda to sustain me, was more than I could face. I came to the decision that I had to talk to Brannigan. I must explain everything to him. He was my only hope, but I couldn't wait until Tuesday when he was expected back at the bank. Sometime tonight, I must alert Manson that men were in the vault, but before doing this, I must talk to Brannigan. I had to find him, and find him fast.

I knew his home telephone number. Forgetting, in my anxiety, that the time was only 07.50, I dialled Brannigan's number. There was a long delay, then a woman's sleepy voice demanded, 'Who is this for God's sake?'

I had met Brannigan's wife several times at cocktail parties: a tall, fifty-year-old, clinging to her youth, jet-black tinted hair, lean and madly interested in her health. I recognised her voice.

'Mrs Brannigan, excuse me. This is Larry Lucas. I …'

'Larry Lucas?' Her voice shot up a notch. 'Well, for God's sake! I haven't seen you in months! How are you, Larry? Wonderful, I'm sure. God! How I wish I could say the same.' Once Merle Brannigan got talking, it was impossible to stop her. 'You wicked man! You woke me up! Now, let me tell you something, Larry. I can't remember when I've had a good night's sleep. You know what I mean? A *good* night's sleep. I get pains in my knees, and there's Farrell snoring his head off, and I lie awake, hour after hour, with pains in my knees every goddamn night. Isn't that something? I talked to Dr Schruder, and he says I walk too much. What a thing to say! I scarcely put one foot before the other. Walk! That's a four-letter word to me!' She gave a trilling laugh. 'What do you think, Larry? Farrell says I'm hysterical. Just imagine that. Hysterical! Last night, right against my will, and I'll let you know, Larry, I really have a very strong will, but right against my will, I took three of those valium – is that what you call them? – anyway, three sleeping pills. And what do you know? Those goddamn pills actually kept me awake! They did absolutely nothing for me, and do you know what I did? The pain was terrible, but in sheer desperation, I got right out of bed, and I went on my knees. God! How I suffered, but I did it, and I talked this problem over with God. Do you believe in God, Larry – of course you do! Well, I talked my problem over with God, and then I got back to bed, and for the first time in

159

months, I went right off to sleep, and now you, you wicked man, have woke me up.'

'Mrs Brannigan,' I said, trying to keep from yelling at her. 'I'm truly sorry about waking you up, but I must contact Mr Brannigan. It's a bank emergency.'

'You want to speak to Farrell?'

I closed my eyes, feeling sweat running down my face.

'Yes, Mrs Brannigan.'

'Did you say it's an emergency?'

'Yes, Mrs Brannigan. I must contact Mr Brannigan.'

'It's Saturday, isn't it, Larry? It's not Monday, is it? God! I'm not awake yet. If it's Monday, I have a date with my hairdresser at nine. Now, isn't that a terrible time to have to go to a hairdresser? He's just so busy ...'

'It is Saturday!' My voice turned into a shout.

'Larry, dear, please don't shout. My nerves are all on edge. If it's Saturday ... how can there be a bank emergency? The bank closes on Saturday ... at least, I think it does.'

Somehow, I controlled my voice.

'I must contact Mr Brannigan. Can you tell me where I can reach him?'

'He's off somewhere, playing golf. You know FB. When he isn't making money, he's playing golf. I remember once, when we were talking to Jerry Ford, Farrell said ...'

'Mrs Brannigan! I am asking for your help! Have you any idea where I can contact Mr Brannigan?'

'He never tells me anything.' Her voice turned sulky. 'You know, sometimes Farrell is very inconsiderate, but I guess most husbands, after they've been married for twenty-five years, get inconsiderate.'

'So you don't know where I can contact him?'

'Well, if it is an emergency – and I can't imagine what emergency – you could ask his secretary. She knows more about my husband's movements than I do. Isn't that terrible? Some chit of a girl knows more ...'

'Thank you, Mrs Brannigan,' and I hung up on her.

I picked up the telephone book, and found Lois Sheldon's home number. A minute later, I was speaking to her.

'This is Larry, Lois. It is urgent that I contact FB. Do you know where he is?'

'How urgent?' Lois' voice was brisk.

'It's an emergency to do with the bank. I can't tell you more than that. FB would want this to be kept top secret, Lois. I must speak to him!'

'I'll see if I can get him. Give me your telephone number. I'll call you back.'

'Can't you give me his telephone number?'

'No. I'll call you back.'

I read off the number on the telephone I was using.

'You are sure this isn't something that can be handled on Monday?' Lois said. 'FB will be wild if I disturb him for nothing.'

'He'll be even wilder if you don't. Hurry it, Lois. I'll wait,' and I hung up.

It was while I was sitting at the desk, I remembered the incriminating photos of Marsh and myself. I began searching the desk drawers. One of them was locked. I went fast into the kitchen in search of tools. I found a long screwdriver in one of the kitchen closets. Returning to the living-room, I attacked the drawer, and in a few minutes, had it open.

Lying in the drawer was the envelope containing the copies of the two tapes and my statement to Brannigan. In yet another envelope were the blackmail photographs showing Marsh and myself fighting, and better yet, the negatives.

I had seen a can of gasoline in the kitchen. I fetched it, then putting the two envelopes into the big fireplace, I soaked them in gasoline, then striking a match, set fire to them.

I stood back, watching the blaze.

When the fire had died down, I stirred the debris, poured on more gasoline, and again threw in a lighted match.

Finally, I was satisfied that nothing now remained of the blackmail pictures nor the tapes and my statement.

Still no telephone call from Lois!

I began searching the closets in the living-room. I came across the trenching tool, wrapped in plastic, that I had handled while they had buried Marsh. I went into the kitchen found a rag, dipped it in water and stripped off the plastic, I wiped the wooden handle free of my fingerprints. Then using the rag, I wiped over the surface of the desk, the arms of the chair and wrapped the rag around the telephone receiver. This was the best I could do.

I looked at my watch. The time now was 08.50. I thought only for a moment of Klaus, Harry, Joe and Benny trapped in the vault, then my mind shifted to Glenda.

I was sitting at the desk, grieving for her, when the telephone bell broke up my thoughts.

I snatched up the receiver. It was Lois.

'Larry, I'm sorry, but I can get no reply,' she said. 'I've called three times. He's either not answering the telephone or he isn't there.'

'Keep trying,' I said feverishly. 'This is a real emergency, Lois. I'll wait.'

'I can't! My mother is sick, and I have to go to her. I have only a few minutes before I get my train!'

'Then give me the number! I'll keep trying!'

'I can't do that!' A pause, then she went on, 'Larry! He's not playing golf! Every so often he goes off for a long weekend, but he doesn't play golf. I don't have to spell it out, do I?'

This shook me. I had always imagined Farrell Brannigan was above the way so many men lived.

'I don't give a damn! I must talk to him, Lois! A situation has come up that could cause a hell of a stink at the bank! I can't tell you more than that, but I have to talk to him, and immediately!'

'But he's not answering!' There was a wail in her voice. 'It would be a breach of confidence if I gave you the number.'

'He'll thank you. I swear he will!' I was shouting now. 'You know he trusts me! This is an emergency! Now, come on, Lois! Give me the number!'

There was a long pause, then she said, 'It's 333 4 77 880. I must go or I'll miss my train,' and she hung up.

I scribbled the number down on a memo pad, lying on the desk. 333 was the code number of Pennon Bay, a small beach resort some ten miles from Sharnville. Bill Dixon and I had once considered renting one of the many beach cabins there with the idea that we could work together Sundays, and sunbathe at the same time. I had gone down there, but had decided there were too many screaming children around to allow us to work in peace. I remembered the Bay: sand, sea, palm trees, well-appointed bungalows, and a couple of decent restaurants. When I had inspected a few of the bungalows with the estate agent, I had thought many of them could be love nests, although most of them were weekend family accommodations. The more isolated bungalows, which I was sure were love nests, the agent told me regretfully weren't for rent.

My hands unsteady, I picked up the telephone book and flicked through the pages until I came to Pennon Bay. There were not more than two hundred entries. Carefully I went down the list of numbers until I came to 4 77 880.

Miss Sheila Vance, 14, Sea Road.

Brannigan's mistress?

Picking up the telephone receiver, I dialled the number. I listened to the ringing tone for over a minute, then I hung up. I looked at my watch. The time now was 09.25.

I had to see Brannigan! I had to throw this whole mess into his lap! I was beyond caring what would happen to me. I couldn't care less if he took the occasional weekend away from his wife, and found consolation with another woman. He had done so much for me in the past, and I felt that if I told him the whole sick story, he would help me ... no one else could!

Leaving the house, I ran to my car, climbed in and started the engine. As I reversed to drive down the dirt road, I thought of the four men, trapped in the vault, then I thought of Glenda. Well, they were trapped. At least, her murder would be avenged!

At the end of the dirt road, I had a long, impatient wait before I could drive on to the highway. Already families were driving to the beaches. The usual Saturday morning exodus from Sharnville was on.

Finally, I was on the highway, but my progress was slow. Cars, with inflated rubber boats strapped to their roofs, were almost bumper to bumper. Kids, leaning out of car windows, screamed and yelled, anticipating the excitement of the sea. Bored-looking husbands, sitting behind the driving wheels, turned, from time to time, to swear at their children, while harassed-looking mothers, dragged the kids back to their seats. It was a typical Sharnville Saturday morning.

Ahead, were Hampton Bay, Bay Creek, Little Cove, Happy Bay, and then Pennon Bay.

The most popular Bay was Little Cove. Once past the turn-off to Little Cove, the traffic thinned and I could increase speed. Only one car signalled to turn left at Pennon Bay. I followed it down the sandy road that led to the beach.

The car, ahead of me, pulled up outside a *de luxe* bungalow, facing the sea, and four kids tumbled out, and ran yelling across the sand while the driver got out to open the gate leading to the garage.

I kept on until I reached a parking bay, then got out of my car. I had no idea where to find Sea Road. I looked right and left, then seeing a youngish man in swim shorts coming my way, I stopped him and asked.

'Sea Road?' He was overweight, and had a mat of black hair on his chest. He looked as intelligent as an amputated leg. 'Sea Road?' He scratched his hairy chest. 'Yeah ... Sea Road.' He frowned. 'Yeah ... you go straight ahead, turn left, and you're on it.'

'Thanks,' I said.

'You're welcome. Have a nice day,' and he plodded away towards the sea.

I started off down the road, then as I was about to turn left, I heard a voice calling. I stopped and turned.

The hairy-chested man was running after me.

'Bud, I'm sorry. You want Sea Road ... right?'

The sun was now up, and in my city clothes, I was sweating.

'Yes.'

'My error, bud. You turn right.'

I could have strangled him.

'You mean I go back to the intersection, and take the right-hand road?'

165

He scratched his chest, frowned, then nodded.

'Yep. You've got it, bud.'

As I started back, he said, 'You got kids, bud?'

Without pausing, I said no.

'If you knew how lucky you are ...' His voice faded away as I kept on.

The bungalows along this beach road were more *de luxe* than the others I had passed. They stood in fair-sized gardens which were screened either by laurel hedges or stone walls. None of the bungalows had numbers: just names like The Nest, Happy Home, You & Me: crazy names people dream up for their houses.

I had walked some hundred yards when I came upon a teenage girl, swinging on the gate leading to a big bungalow. She was pencil thin, fair, and wore jeans and a sweat shirt. She regarded me with worldly eyes and an impish grin.

'Hello,' she said.

I paused.

'I'm looking for 14, Sea Road.'

Her grin turned to a sly little smile.

'Are you looking for Sheila?'

'That's right. Do you know her?'

She pouted.

'My mum won't let me talk to her. I say hello to her when my mum's not around.'

Fishing for information, I asked, 'What's your mum got against her?'

The girl wrinkled her nose.

'My mum's square. Just because Sheila has a boyfriend or two, my mum says she's a whore.'

'Where do I find her place?'

Again the sly little smile.

'If I were you, I wouldn't go there right now. She's got her fat friend with her. He's old and horrid looking, but her real boyfriend is super. When Sheila doesn't want to swim, he comes swimming with me ... when my mum's not around,' and she giggled.

Still fishing, I asked, 'How do you know he is her real boyfriend. Her fat friend could be her real boyfriend, couldn't he?'

'That's a load of crap. The fat one comes only once a month, but Harry lives with her.'

'Harry?'

I felt a cold chill run over me. Then I told myself Harry was a common name, but instinct warned me to probe.

'Harry ... tall, thin with a beard?'

Her eyes opened wide.

'Sure ... do you know him?' Holding the gate with one hand as she swung backwards and forwards, she tossed her long fair hair off her shoulders. 'What's your name? How did you meet Harry?'

'You haven't told me where I can find Sheila.'

'Right at the end of the road. It's the only bungalow with a number. When did you meet Harry?'

A raucous voice bawled from somewhere: 'Jenny! Come in at once!'

The girl grimaced.

'That's my mum. See you,' and climbing off the gate, she ran away towards the bungalow.

As I started down the sandy road, I was asking myself what was going on. I told myself I mustn't jump to conclusions. There could be hundreds of bearded men called Harry.

My mind in a turmoil, I hurried on. At the end of the road was a high laurel hedge, screening a bungalow. On the gate was the number 14. I pushed open the gate and looked into the big garden. Ahead of me, up a crazy path was a low-lying, biggish bungalow. I walked quickly up the path until I reached the front door.

What kind of reception would I receive when Brannigan found I had tracked him down to his love nest? I hesitated for a brief moment, then thumbed the bell push.

Somewhere inside the bungalow, I heard a bell ring. Then, after a brief moment, the door jerked open.

Standing in the doorway, wearing white pyjamas, her red hair tousled, her big, green eyes wide, was Glenda.

A bunch of kids, dressed in cowboy outfits, burst into the garden. The toy guns they carried were perfect replicas of the real thing. As they shot at each other, the snapping bark of their guns was horribly realistic.

Two of the kids fell down, cluching at their chests, their legs jerking as they simulated violent death. One of the other kids, his face snarling, ran over to them and shot at them, screaming: 'You're dead ... you're dead!'

Then leaving the two, now lying still, the rest of them charged back on to the road, and went, yelling, towards the sea.

The sight of Glenda, with this sudden invasion of noise, paralysed me. I could only stand motionless, staring at her, seeing the two kids get to their feet.

One pointed his gun at me and fired.

'You're dead!' he yelled, fired again, then he and his companion charged after the others.

'Glenda!' I managed to say.

Her face was the colour of tallow. Her eyes were terror stricken. Slowly, she backed away as if she were seeing a ghost, her hand to her mouth. She half moaned to herself: 'Oh, my God! My God!'

'Glenda!'

I took a step forward.

With a stifled scream, she turned and stumbled down the long passage, threw open the door on her right, stumbled inside the room and slammed the door.

My mind wouldn't work. I stood in the doorway, unable to move. I had been so sure Klaus had had her murdered. The shock of finding her alive, and even worse, the realisation that the sight of me had reduced her to terrifying panic, crushed me.

I stood there, looking down the passage at the closed door behind which she was. Somewhere in the bungalow a clock began to chime. Standing there, feeling the sun on my back, I counted the chimes. It was now 11.00. The clock chimes brought my mind into focus. I moved into the passage, and closed the front door. I walked down the passage, reached the door to the room where Glenda was, turned the handle, but found the door locked.

'Glenda!' I shouted. 'Let me in! You have nothing to be frightened about. Glenda ... please!'

A gravelly voice said, behind me, 'Leave her alone, Larry. She's had a shock.'

I spun around.

Farrell Brannigan stood in the passage. He was wearing a white open-neck shirt and blue slacks. Although casually dressed, he still exuded all the authority of the President of the largest banking syndicate in California.

'Come on, son,' he said. 'We have things to talk about. Just let her alone for a while. Women need to get over a shock like this.'

Bewildered, and off balance, I hesitated, then followed him into the big living-room, comfortably furnished with lounging chairs, settees and a big desk.

'Now, Larry,' Brannigan said quietly as he moved behind the desk, 'just so you don't get wrong ideas about Glenda and myself, I will tell you in confidence that she is my illegitimate daughter.'

I stared at him, feeling a wave of relief go through me. His daughter! My reaction, when I had seen her standing in the doorway, had been that she was Sheila Vance ... Brannigan's mistress.

'Your daughter?' I said, continuing to stare at him.

He dropped into the big chair behind the desk, then took a cigar from a box as he waved me to a chair. 'Come on, Larry, sit down. I've some history to tell you.'

Even more bewildered, I sat down. He was as calm as if he were presiding at a board meeting.

'I'm going to tell you something in strict confidence, Larry,' he went on. 'Not a word to anyone else. I know I can trust you. Right?'

'Glenda is your daughter?'

He nodded.

'That's it. Glenda's mother was a secretary of mine. This was twenty-six years ago.' He puffed smoke. 'I had been married for a few months. Merle, as you know, is occupied with her health. She never gave me any bed satisfaction.' He pointed his cigar at me. 'A man wants bed satisfaction. That's what marriage is all about. That, and companionship.' He drew on his cigar, then went on, 'What no one knows, Larry, is that it is Merle's money that gave me my start. I'm putting the cards on the table. If she wasn't so rich, I wouldn't have married her. I wanted money, so I married her. Merle was difficult. She is one of these women who is above sex. I got nothing from her, so, after a while, I began to screw around. What man wouldn't? Let's look at it, Larry. There are two things in a man's life: money and screwing.'

As I didn't say anything, he went on, 'Stupidly, I screwed my secretary, Anne, Glenda's mother. Anne was a nice girl ... a decent girl. She died giving birth to Glenda.' He heaved a sigh. 'I found I had a baby daughter on my hands. I knew if Merle heard about it, she would divorce me, and I would lose her financial backing. I wanted my daughter. Merle would never give me children. I found two worthy people to take care of Glenda, and from time to time, I saw her.' He puffed more smoke. 'You probably won't realise how a man feels when he has a daughter, but never mind. You could learn. I saw Glenda once a month as she grew up. She lacked for nothing. I gave her the best education. I even taught her to play golf. I bought her this place so we could meet from time to time. We met at some out-of-the-way golf course, and played. Then something went wrong. Maybe, she didn't see enough of me. There were times when I was so goddamn busy, I didn't see her more than three times a year. I don't know, but something went wrong. This man Harry Brett came into her life. I knew sooner or later, someone would come, but I hoped that whoever it was, he would be better than Brett. Whenever I can, I come here, and spend a weekend with her, as I'm doing now. I alert her, and she gets rid of Brett.' He moved back his chair and crossed one heavy leg over the other. 'Now, there's a change, Larry.' He looked at me soberly, the relaxed President at the board table, his cigar between his thick fingers, expensive Havana smoke in the air. 'A big change,' he went on. 'She is now in love with you. She doesn't want Brett any more. She wants you.' He leaned forward to touch off the ash from his cigar into the ash bowl. 'At the moment, son, the situation is difficult, but I feel sure you and I can sort it out. What you must keep in mind is that my daughter loves you, needs you, and relies on you to help her and help me.'

For a long moment, I sat silent. I looked at this big, impressive man, and I felt a despairing sickness as it dawned on me he was lying. Farrell Brannigan! The man, who, with a wave of his hand, had done so much for me. My mind flashed back to the past few weeks. Marsh murdered. Thomson, murdered. The blackmail threat. Klaus, Benny, Joe and Harry Brett. Glenda pleading for me to tell them how to break into the bank. Her faked captivity. The impish smile from the teenager as she swung on the gate, when she spoke of Harry Brett.

Keeping my face expressionless, I asked, 'You are saying Glenda relies on me to help you. How can I possibly help you, Mr Brannigan? Why should a man of your status need my help?'

His eyes shifted from me to the wall behind me, and back to me again.

'Do I have to remind you, Larry, if it wasn't for me, you would still be a mechanic? Because of me, you now own a flourishing business, and you are regarded as an important citizen in Sharnville ... because of me.'

I continued to look directly at him, saying nothing.

After a long pause, he went on, 'I need your help, Larry, as you once needed my help. This thing has developed into a dangerous mess. You, and only you, can straighten it out. Both Glenda and I are relying on your help.'

'What thing, Mr Brannigan?'

His fatherly smile became fixed. He rubbed his jaw, pulled at his cigar, then released a cloud of smoke that half screened his face.

'Larry, we both are relying on you. I brought you from nothing. Don't you think you can return favour for favour?'

'I ask again, Mr Brannigan, what thing has developed into a dangerous mess?'

A faint flush came to his heavy face. He sat upright. He was now no longer the father figure, but the tough President, up against opposition.

'We're wasting time, son!' There was a snap in his voice. 'You know very well what I'm talking about! Don't fence with me! What has happened at the bank?'

Then I knew, just by looking at the hard eyes, that Farrell Brannigan was involved in the bank break-in. By now, I was shockproof, and my mind was working actively.

'You needn't worry about the bank, Mr Brannigan,' I said. 'Four evil men are trapped in the vault. There is no possible way for them to get out unless I get them out. I guaranteed to build you the safest bank in the world ... it is the safest bank in the world.'

Slowly, he crushed out his cigar in the ash bowl. Beneath his heavy golfer's tan, his complexion turned yellow.

'You're telling me they are trapped in the vault?' His voice was now husky. I could see his confidence oozing away.

'It is the safest bank in the world, Mr Brannigan. When a psychopath, and three morons, one a vicious killer, try to break into your bank which I built, they become trapped.'

He reached for another cigar, and I saw his hand was unsteady, then he changed his mind, withdrew his hand, then looked at me.

'But you can get them out, Larry?'

'Yes, I could get them out,' I said, 'but I don't intend to.' I leaned forward, then asked, 'Do you want them to escape, Mr Brannigan?'

He sat still, and I could see him visibly shrinking. He was now no longer the President of the biggest banking syndicate in California: he was an ageing, fat man whom I could no longer respect.

'They must escape, Larry,' he said, finally, his voice a husky whisper.

'They are not going to escape,' I said. 'My next move is to telephone Manson, and warn him there are four bank robbers locked in the vault. Once he has alerted the police, I will go down to the bank, and open the vault. The way I've fixed it, no one, except me, can do this. It is still the safest bank in the world.'

I got up and walked over to the desk and reached for the telephone. As I picked up the receiver, the door slammed open, and Glenda rushed in.

She was now wearing green slacks and a white shirt. In her hand, she held an automatic pistol. She pointed the gun at me.

'Get away from that phone!' she screamed.

There was a mad look of frenzy in her eyes. Her mouth was working, the gun wavered in her hand.

I took two steps away from the desk.

'Glenda!' Brannigan's voice was sharp.

She looked at him, her eyes loathing.

'There is no one now, Glenda, except Larry, who can help us,' Brannigan said, his voice pleading. 'Don't do anything dramatic.'

I was looking at her, seeing the hard, drawn face, the vicious, angry eyes, and I didn't recognise this woman I believed I loved. The woman whose soft yielding body had received me, whose pleading voice had begged me to save her life, had vanished, to be replaced by this red-headed, dangerous-looking woman whom the teenager's mother had called a whore.

Although I thought I was, by now, shockproof, the realisation that Glenda had used me so heartlessly and ruthlessly, sickened me.

'What have you done with Harry?' she demanded, her voice shrill. 'What have you done with him, you sonofabitch?'

'Glenda!' Brannigan shouted. 'Go away! Leave this to me! Hear me?'

She looked at him, her big eyes scornful.

'Don't tell me what to do, you fat sack of crap! Your daughter! That's a laugh! Do you imagine you can talk this smart bastard into believing your lies?' Turning on me, 'You're going to get Harry out of that vault!' She waved the gun at me. 'If you don't, I'll kill you!'

'Go ahead and shoot me, Glenda,' I said quietly. 'No one but me can open that vault, and the air is running out. In another four or five hours, your Harry, and the rest of them, will suffocate to death. This is up to you. Go ahead and shoot!'

She moved back, her hand going to her mouth.

'Suffocate?'

'There is no ventilation now in the vault,' I said. 'Right now, four men are using up the remaining air ... it won't last long.' I held out my hand. 'I'll get him out, but on my own terms. Give me that gun!'

'You're bluffing, you devil!'

'You called Klaus that, didn't you? Give me that gun!'

'Give it to him!' Brannigan shouted.

She hesitated, then threw the gun at my feet.

'Take it!' she screamed at me. 'You and your cheap love! Harry is ten times the man you are!' and she ran out of the room, slamming the door.

I picked up the gun and laid it on the desk, then moving slowly, I returned to my chair and sat down.

There was a long pause, then Brannigan said uneasily, 'She's hysterical, Larry. You know what women are.'

I looked up, my fists clenched.

Your cheap, stupid love!

That hurt, but now I knew the truth. All along Brannigan had been lying. The scornful way she had said *Your daughter!* told me she was his mistress, and the lies he had told me about his secretary had been futile attempts to keep some gilt over his image.

'So, according to you,' I said, 'she loves me. What a liar you are!'

He flinched.

'Is it true these men could suffocate?' he asked.

'At a guess, they have another six hours. Dixon and I built that vault. There is a ventilation fan, but to get out of the vault, I had to cut the electricity. I don't bluff, and I don't tell lies.'

He nodded wearily: an old, fat man, shrunken and defeated.

On the desk was a tape recorder.

'Mr Brannigan, I want the truth from you,' I said, 'No more lies. I am going to take a recording of what we say to each other.'

'Don't do that, son,' he said. 'You're telling me I'm at the end of my road.'

'That's what I am telling you,' and I pressed the start button of the recorder. 'You told me Glenda was your daughter. That was a lie?'

'Yes, son, that was a lie. She's my mistress. She has a fatal attraction. Let me tell you, Larry, she's made a lot of money out of me.'

'She told me she was married to Alex Marsh ... right or wrong?'

'She was never married to him ... he was her pimp. He was blackmailing me. He had photographs of Glenda with me ... photographs that were so damning that Merle would have divorced me if she had seen them. Without Merle's money, I am in financial trouble. I paid heavy blackmail to Marsh. Sooner or later, I knew Merle would question me about this steady drain on her fortune. I had to do something to stop Marsh.' Brannigan eased his bulk back in his chair, then went on, 'Marsh was infatuated with Glenda as I was, but he was greedy. Glenda knew he was blackmailing me, but Marsh, like the pimp he was, never gave her a cent of the money he was getting from me.

'Marsh suspected that I could be dangerous. He knew I would try to get the photos, and then have him murdered. A few weeks ago, he came to me. "Mr Brannigan," he said, "don't get ideas about getting those photos and having me knocked off. Those photos are in a safe deposit box in the safest bank in the world," and he grinned at me. "My lawyer holds the key of the box. If anything happens to me, the box will be opened, and you can then explain the photographs to your wife." I realised there was nothing I could do about this. Marsh had played it very smart.' Brannigan paused to wipe his sweating face with the back of his hand. 'There was no way, even for the President of the bank, to get at Marsh's deposit box.' He stared at me, his eyes dull. 'You made that impossible.' There was a pause, then he said, 'I could do with a drink, son.'

I got up and went to the liquor cabinet and built him a powerful whisky and soda. He took the glass with a shaky hand, drank, sighed, then put the glass down.

'So my future life,' he went on, 'was locked up in the vault you built, Larry. I desperately wanted to be financially independent, instead of relying on my wife's money. There was a big deal pending, and this could be my chance. By using Merle's credit, I could get in on the ground floor. Then just when I was fixing this deal, Marsh reappeared. He said he had decided to leave the States. He demanded two million dollars as final blackmail payment, and he would give me the photographs and the negatives. He said he would give me two weeks to raise the money, then, if I didn't pay him, he would go to Merle who, he was sure, would pay up to avoid a scandal. She wouldn't have paid up. She would have divorced me and my future would be ended.' He sat forward, his big hands turning into fists. 'Then I realised there was only one possible solution out of this mess. I had to find some criminal who would break into the bank, get me those photographs and murder Marsh. This was my only solution.' He paused to sip his drink. 'I had no contacts with the criminal world. In my position, I couldn't go around trying to find a bank robber, then I remembered Klaus. Now, Klaus ...'

'You can skip that,' I interrupted. 'I have it already on tape. Years ago, you and he worked together, you found he had embezzled, and you got him a five-year sentence ... right?'

He looked down at his tightly clenched fists.

'That's what happened. At that time, I believed anyone working in a bank must be honest. When there is no pressure, it is easy to be honest.'

'So you found Klaus, and you asked him to break into the bank?'

'There was no one else I could go to.' He finished his drink. 'You must understand, Larry, I was now desperate. My whole life depended on getting Marsh off my back ...

to get those photographs. After I had talked to Klaus, I realised he was a mental case. Maybe the years he had spent in jail had eroded his mind. He hated me. I could see his hatred oozing out of him while we talked. He had read all the media about my safest bank in the world. It delighted him that he would break into the bank and make a sham of me. "I'll get your photographs," he said, "but remember, every banker in the world will be laughing at you! I'll cut you down to size!" That was how his sick mind worked.' Brannigan pushed his empty glass towards me. 'I would like another, son.'

I got up and built him another drink, and gave it to him. 'Thanks.' He sipped the drink, then went on, 'I didn't give a damn about the bank. That's where Klaus made a mistake. He imagined he was punishing me. I had to get those photographs. If there was one man in the world who could break into the bank, it was Klaus. The deal we agreed to was for the men he employed to have the contents of the deposit boxes, for me to get the photographs, and for Klaus to satisfy his pathological hatred of me to prove to the world I didn't own the safest bank in the world.' He lifted his heavy hands and let them drop with a thud on the desk. 'That's the sordid story, Larry. I've levelled with you. Can you get me out of this mess?'

I thought back to the time when we had first met, when I had fixed his putting and his hook. I thought of his influence that had made me an important citizen in Sharnville. Then, to me, he had been a great man, but not now. Looking at him, seated in the chair, sweat running down his heavy face, Farrell Brannigan ceased to be the god I thought he was.

'You haven't levelled with me,' I said. 'You know as well as I do Klaus could never have broken into the bank. You knew I was the only man in the world to do that! So you set me up.'

He moved restlessly.

'Now, look, son …'

'Don't give me this son routine! Didn't you tell Klaus I was the sucker who could get him into the bank?'

He rubbed his sweating face.

'I guess.' He tried to drag a shred of dignity over himself. 'I did mention …'

'You did more than that! Now, I'll tell you what you did! You knew Klaus hadn't a hope in hell to break into the bank, so you set me up. I was to be the sucker! You and your son routine! You didn't give a damn about me. All you thought of was to hang on to your image. You planted Glenda on me! That crap about Joe going to your place and putting water in your gas tank was just another lie I was fed with. You gambled that I would fall for Glenda, and I did. Her supposed reportage on Sharnville paid off. She not only threw a hook into me, she also alerted Klaus that the Sheriff was dangerous, and Manson was incorruptible. So what happened? The Sheriff was murdered. Don't tell me you didn't know what was happening! Don't tell me you didn't know Klaus was pinning Marsh's murder on me! You once said to me you liked to play God … what a god!'

He waved his big hands as if trying to push away the truth.

'I swear to you, Larry! I left everything to Klaus!'

I looked at him in disgust.

'You would swear to anything to save your rotten image.' I stopped the tape recorder and pressed the rewind button. 'At least, I have a chance, but you haven't. I am now going to the police. With this tape, and the other tapes I have, I stand a chance.' I lifted the spool off the sprocket and dropped the spool into my pocket. 'This is the end of your road. I'll leave you the gun.'

'Wait, Larry!' There was a desperate urgency in his voice. 'We can still fix this. All I ask you is hold everything until tomorrow. We two, together, can work a way out of this mess.'

I regarded him.

'In another few hours, long before tomorrow, four men will die of suffocation. Do you want that?'

'Don't you see, son? A madman, and three enemies of society! Who cares what happens to them?' He pounded his fists on his desk. 'With them out of the way, there are no witnesses. If they haven't broken into Marsh's deposit box, then it doesn't matter. If they have found the photographs, I know the shape of the envelope. I'll be there when Manson opens the vault, and I'll get the photographs! Larry! I raised you from nothing! Be grateful! Do this for me!'

The sound of a car starting up made us both stiffen.

'What's that?' Brannigan demanded.

'No witnesses? At a guess, I think Glenda has been listening to what you have been saying, and she is now on her way to try and rescue Harry.'

He got unsteadily to his feet.

'Stop her!'

He lurched to his feet, gun in hand and jerked open the front door.

His Cadillac was racing down the sandy road. Brannigan raised the gun. I caught hold of his wrist, and forced the gun down.

'This is the end of the road for you,' I said. 'Now it's your chance to play god with God,' and I left him, and began my long walk back to my car.

The teenager was swinging on the gate as I approached.

181

'Hello,' she said, with her impish grin. 'Did you see her?' She hung on to the gate while she lifted her hair off her face. 'She went by just now.'

The distant snap of gunfire came over the sound of her childish voice, over the slap of the sea on the beach, and over the screech of gulls.

I paused.

She cocked her head on one side.

'That was a gun,' she said. 'Someone shooting! How exciting!'

I thought of Brannigan. I thought again of all he had done for me. I thought of his ruthlessness. A bullet through a head can solve every problem.

'You've been watching too much television,' I said, my voice husky, and I walked on to my car.

On the drive back to Sharnville, I banished Brannigan from my mind. As I got into my car, I hoped the sound of gunfire I had heard meant he was free of his wife, free of his ruthlessness, and that the credit and debit balance of his life would add up on the credit side.

I now had to think of myself. I had some five hours before the air in the vault became exhausted. Before I alerted the police, I had to talk to Manson. He was now my last hope.

Driving along the highway, I glanced at my watch. The time now was 13.00. I had no idea how Manson spent his weekends. I imagined he was the kind of man to spend his off days with his wife and his two children, probably pottering in the garden.

Seeing a café-bar, I pulled up and shut myself in one of the telephone booths. I didn't want to waste time driving out to Manson's home, which was on the east side of Sharnville, only to find him out.

I dialled his number and listened to the ringing tone, then just as I was beginning to think he was out, there was a click, then Manson said, 'Who is this?'

'Larry Lucas.'

'Oh, Larry.' His voice lifted a note. 'Hold a moment.' I heard him say something indistinctly. He probably had his hand over the mouthpiece. 'Will you come out here quickly, Larry?'

From the urgency in his voice, I knew Glenda had played it smart. I should have thought of Manson.

'Hostage, Alec?' I asked quietly.

'Yes. Just come out here. Don't do anything. You understand? Just come.' The strain in his voice came over the line.

'I'm on my way,' I said, and hung up.

I could imagine the scene: Manson, his wife and his two kids facing a gun held by Glenda.

I hesitated. Should I alert the police? *Don't do anything.* There had been a desperate plea in Manson's voice.

I remembered Glenda as she threatened me with the gun: *You are going to get Harry out of that vault! If you don't, I'll kill you!* I remembered the vicious, murderous glare in her green eyes.

This wasn't the time for the police.

Leaving the café-bar at a run, I got into my car, and headed fast down the highway. At this hour, most people were on the beach or in restaurants, so I had a clear run, but I took no chances. I kept just within the speed limit, but only just.

As I pulled into the drive leading to Manson's house, I saw Brannigan's Cadillac parked by the front door, then I knew for certain that Glenda was in the house with a gun.

I got out of my car, and walked fast around the Caddy, and up to the front door which opened as I arrived at the top of the steps.

Manson stood facing me. We stared at each other. I found it hard to recognise this tall, thin man, wearing a blue cotton shirt and white slacks: the man I had come to regard as an efficient, impersonal banker. Before me, was a terrified, sweating wreck of a man whose mouth twitched, whose eyes were dull with shock.

'For Christ's sake!' he shouted at me. 'What's happening? This woman is threatening to kill my children! She wants me to open the vault! I've told her over and over again, I can't do it until Monday morning!'

'But you can, you sonofabitch!' Glenda cried from the living-room doorway. 'Come in here!'

Manson, trembling, moved to one side, and I walked into the living-room.

I was confronted by the scene I expected.

On the big settee was Monica Manson, her arms around her two small children. I had met Monica at the occasional banker's cocktail party. She was a nice, housewife type: entirely suitable for Manson. The two children, a boy and a girl, looked scared. The girl was crying.

Glenda backed away. She was holding a small automatic rifle that could be deadly at any range. She looked devilish as she glared at me.

'You're opening the vault!' she shrilled. 'You're going to get Harry out!' She turned to Monica. 'If you want to see your fink of a husband alive, do nothing! You alert the cops, and I'll blow his goddamn head off!' She swung the gun to cover me. 'Let's go!' The gun moved to Manson. 'You too!'

Then I realised she was making the same mistake that Klaus had made when he had joined in the bank raid. If Glenda had used her head, she would have realised her position was unassailable if she stayed with Monica and the children. Threatening to kill them would have given me no room in which to manoeuvre. I would have had to open the vault, but she was so worked up, she didn't seem to realise she was throwing away her trump card.

Not giving her a chance to change her thinking, I caught hold of Manson's arm and half dragged him out into the hot sunshine.

'Leave this to me! Say nothing!' I whispered urgently as I heard Glenda scream at Monica not to do a thing.

I was now calmly cold. Poor Manson was in such a state, I had to hold on to his arm to steady him.

'We'll use my car,' I said to Glenda. 'I have all my tools in the trunk.'

'Listen, smart ass,' she said, 'you try anything tricky with me, and I'll blow his goddamn head off! You drive. He sits with you! Get moving!'

We got into the car; Glenda at the back, the gun barrel nudging Manson's neck.

'Hurry it up, damn you!' she screamed at me.

I drove fast to the highway, and headed for Sharnville's Main Street.

'Glenda, listen to me,' I said quietly. 'I'll get Harry out, but this is the end of your road and his. Brannigan shot himself.'

I heard Manson catch his breath sharply, but he had the sense to keep silent.

'It could still be a long road, you sonofabitch,' Glenda said. 'I don't give a damn about Brannigan. There's only one man in my life, and that's Harry! If we're going, we'll go together, and this fink and you'll go with us! Make no mistake about that!'

I slowed as we approached Main Street. Looking ahead, I saw the bank guard, his rifle slung over his shoulder, standing outside his sentry-box. There were few cars on the street: not more than a dozen people were wandering aimlessly, shop window gazing.

I pulled up in front of the bank.

The guard straightened, peered, then recognised Manson, he gave him a salute, then he saw Glenda's gun. His round, middle-aged face turned the colour of mutton fat. He clawed at his gun. The hammering sound of the automatic rifle exploded in my ears as Glenda shot him.

'Out!' she screamed. 'Get the bank open!'

Shocked, I slid out of the car, ran around, opened the trunk and grabbed up the plastic sack. My hands were shaking as I found the neutraliser, aware people were shouting. As I pushed the button on the neutraliser, and as the bank doors swung open, I saw a cop running down the street, gun in hand. He paused, stared at us, recognised Manson, then saw Glenda's gun. He fatally hesitated as she fired a short burst at him. He went down, clutching his chest.

'Get in!' she screamed, and herded Manson and me into the bank. 'Shut the doors!'

I flicked the neutraliser, and the bank doors closed.

'Where's the vault?' she demanded.

'Over there,' and I pointed.

She ran through the invisible alarm beam to the vault doors. By breaking the beam, she had unwittingly alerted the Sharnville station house, the Federal Bureau's local office and the Los Angeles police. Within minutes, every available policeman in the district would be surrounding the bank.

She hammered on the vault door with the butt of her gun, screaming, 'Harry! I'll get you out! Hear me, Harry!'

I grabbed Manson's arm and hissed to him, 'When I say run, run like hell and hide!'

Glenda spun around, glaring at me.

'Open up or he'll get it,' and her gun shifted to Manson.

'To open the vault, the lock releases are on the second floor,' I said, and moving to the elevator, I used the neutraliser.

The elevator doors swished open, and I stepped inside.

For a brief moment, she hesitated, then shoving Manson forward into the cage, she followed him.

Another mistake! If she had stayed with Manson in the bank's lobby, I would have been hamstrung.

This was an automatic elevator. There wasn't a lot of room. While she was shoving Manson against the side of the cage, I pressed the second floor button, and then the fourth floor button.

This was a deadly risk, but a good chance.

The doors closed, and the elevator rose swiftly to the second floor, stopped, and the doors opened.

This was my moment of truth!

My heart was pounding as I watched Glenda back out of the elevator, covering Manson and myself with the gun.

'Come out!' she shouted.

The opening of the elevator cage was narrow. Before Manson could move, I stepped in front of him, moved out of the cage and stood, blocking the entrance.

'Get out of the way!' Glenda screamed, suddenly sensing she had been outwitted.

'Glenda! It's either Harry's life or my life,' I said. 'Shoot me and Harry dies too.'

As I heard the elevator doors close, I shouted, 'Run!'

'You bastard!'

Was she going to shoot? Sweat ran down my back as we faced each other.

'Glenda! I'll open the vault! I'll get Harry out!' I shouted at her.

She looked to right and left, fury, frustration and fear contorted her face. Then seeing the stairs at the end of the corridor, she turned and began to run blindly towards them with the futile hope of catching Manson, her only hostage.

I overtook her in ten long strides, and brought her down, my arms around her waist. The gun flew out of her hands as she thudded to the floor.

She lay there, stunned, while I picked up the gun. Her hands covered her face, and she began to sob.

Over the sounds of her sobbing, came the sound of police sirens as police cars converged on the bank.

Captain Perrell of the LA Police, who had arrived by helicopter, sat behind Manson's desk.

Manson and I sat facing him.

Deputy Sheriff Tim Bentley stood behind Perrell.

Perrell was very much in charge. He was a man who first got his facts right, then made quick decisions.

When I had opened the bank doors, and had let him in with a flock of policemen and plainclothes men, he had asked abruptly what was going on. He eyed the automatic rifle I was holding, and a plainclothes man sidled up, and took it away from me.

'There are four dangerous men trapped in the vault,' I told Perrell.

He absorbed the information without a change of expression.

'There is a woman on the second floor. The gun is hers: she is one of the gang,' I went on. 'She is unarmed, but dangerous.'

Perrell snapped his fingers, and two plainclothes men, drawing their guns, started up the stairs.

I felt a chill around my heart. I had loved Glenda. Maybe there was still a shred of love left.

'These guys in the vault armed?' Perrell demanded.

'Yes, and one of them is a moronic, vicious killer. They are all highly dangerous.'

'Right. We'll go up and take a look at this woman.'

There was drama on the second floor as we emerged from the elevator. One of the plainclothes men was peering around the door of Manson's office. The other was preparing to move in.

'Hold it!' Perrell snapped.

'She's out on the ledge,' the taller of the cops said. 'She's ready to take a dive.'

Through the open window of Manson's office, we heard a loud moan of excitement from the crowd below.

Perrell moved cautiously into the office. I followed him.

Glenda was leaning back against one of the windows, her back to us. She was looking down at the crowded street.

'Let me talk to her,' I said urgently, and pushing by Perrell, I slowly approached the big open window through which she had climbed.

'Glenda!' I spoke gently. 'Come on in. I'm getting Harry out. He'll want to talk to you.'

At the sound of my voice, she looked around. Her face was white, her eyes sunken, her lips drawn back in the snarl of a trapped animal. I had loved this woman, but there was nothing now in her face that had sparked my love. She was a vicious, crazy-looking stranger.

189

'You stinking devil!' she screamed at me. 'Here's yours!'

She lifted a hand, and a small 22 automatic levelled at me.

There was a bang of a gun, just behind me, as Perrell shot her. With horror, I saw blood and a smashed skull as she reeled and fell to the street.

There was confusion. Screams from the street below: men shouting. I staggered over to a chair and sank into it. I heard vaguely, as if in a dream, Perrell snapping orders, but what he was saying didn't register. There was more confusion: men moving around ... voices.

I saw her again on the golf course; remembered the wonderful dinner she had cooked for me; recalled that moment when I had first made love to her: saw her in the bikini, sitting on the sand, waiting to betray me.

'Larry!' Manson's voice jerked me upright. He was standing over me. 'They want me to open the vault! I keep telling them we have to wait until Monday morning!'

I pulled myself together.

'I can open it.'

He stared at me.

'What are you saying?'

'Okay, Lucas,' Perrell said curtly. 'Let's talk it out.'

So, sitting around Manson's desk, I told them. I kept nothing back. I told them the whole story, aware that a cop, sitting in a corner, was taking down every word I was saying. I was past caring. I knew what I was saying would be front-page news tomorrow, and I knew I was finished in Sharnville. At the back of my mind, I thought of Bill Dixon. He would have to find another partner. I just didn't care any more.

When I was through, there was a long pause. Manson was staring at me in shocked horror. I took from my pocket the cassette and pushed it over to Perrell. 'That's

190

Brannigan's statement. His secretary has the other two tapes. Brannigan was in on it from the beginning. You will find his body at 14, Sea Road, Pennon Bay.'

'Hold it!' Perrell snapped. He turned to Bentley. 'Check that out, Tim! Better take an ambulance, and the MO.'

As Bentley hurried out of the office, a police sergeant looked in.

'All set, Captain.'

'I'll take a look.' Perrell got to his feet. 'You come with me, Lucas. If it looks sour, you tell me.'

Leaving Manson who was telephoning his wife, we rode down the elevator to the lobby.

The scene had changed.

Four powerful floodlights were focused on the vault doors with blinding intensity. Five uniformed policemen, wearing flak jackets, and cradling submachine guns, knelt behind the lights, invisible to anyone facing the lights. Some ten policemen stood just outside the bank entrance, also in flak jackets and holding submachine guns.

'Can those men hear through the vault door?' Perrell asked me.

'No.'

'Is there any way to tell them to give up?'

'No.'

He shrugged.

'Well, okay, then it's up to them.' He turned to the five policemen. 'If they start anything, wipe them out.' Then to me, 'Go ahead and open the vault.'

'It'll take some twenty minutes.'

'We're in no hurry,' he snapped. 'Get moving!'

I took the elevator back to the second floor, found the plastic sack, containing my gimmicks and tools I had dropped when confronting Glenda, and walked into Manson's office.

Manson was on his own, much more relaxed now he had talked to his wife. He was once again the efficient, impersonal banker.

'Larry,' he said, 'I now know what it means to come under pressure. Even a man as big as Brannigan cracked under pressure. I want you to know you can rely on me to help you. I am on your side. You saved the lives of my children.'

I scarcely listened. I was thinking of the four men trapped in the vault. Because of my expertise, I could open the vault door. Then what would happen? I thought of the five policemen, crouching, with their guns. Maybe these four men would surrender. Klaus? I didn't think he would want to face a life sentence. No, he wouldn't surrender. Benny? He, I was sure, would come out shooting. Harry and Joe ... maybe they would surrender.

'Don't talk now, Alec,' I said, and got out my tools.

He watched me strip out the wires of the telephone. Because my hands were shaking, it took time. I got the gimmick wired up as Perrell came in.

'The doors will open in whatever time you say,' I told him.

'Give me a minute,' and he left the office at a run.

I gave him two minutes, staring at the second hand of my watch, then I dialled the four numbers, got up, crossed to the cassette slot and pressed down the cassette. Seconds later, the green light came up to signal the vault doors had opened. I ran from the office. As I started down the stairs, I heard gunfire. The noise of the submachine guns opening up was deafening. I ran on down the stairs as more violent gunfire erupted.

It was all over when I reached the lobby.

I had been half right, half wrong.

Klaus lay in a pool of blood. Benny, crouching against the wall, his hands above his head, was screaming. 'Don't shoot! Don't shoot!'

In the centre of the lobby, Joe lay, half curled up, his chest torn to pieces.

With a sick, empty feeling, I remained on the stairs, surveying the scene.

No Harry?

I waited, staring at the open vault.

The police sergeant, crouching behind one of the lights, bawled, 'Come out with your hands on your head!'

Gun smoke drifted around the lobby. There was a long pause, then slowly, his hands on his head, Harry walked into the beams of the lights.

I stared at him: tall, bearded, pale under his tan, sweat running down his face.

The only man in my life, Glenda had said.

Well, at least he was alive. He would probably be in the cage for the rest of his life. Looking at him, I could see there was this thing about him that told me why Glenda had loved him so desperately. He was still cocky, still confident, still undefeated, and I felt sure he would always be the same.

Benny was being hustled away.

Four policemen surrounded Harry, and one of them snapped on handcuffs. Harry looked around and saw me. He managed a pale grin.

'You can't win all the time, can you, buster?' he said. 'Man! Did you play it smart!'

As they began to hustle him away, I moved forward.

'Wait!'

The cops stared at me as I faced Harry.

'Harry, I want you to know Glenda did everything she could to save you. She's dead.'

He stared at me, then sneered.

'That hustler? Who cares if she's dead? She wasn't even a good screw,' and shoving by me, he went with the cops into the hot sunshine.

>>> If you've enjoyed this book and would like to discover more great vintage crime and thriller titles, as well as the most exciting crime and thriller authors writing today, visit: >>>

The Murder Room
Where Criminal Minds Meet

themurderroom.com

>>>

www.ingramcontent.com/pod-product-compliance
Ingram Content Group UK Ltd.
Pitfield, Milton Keynes, MK11 3LW, UK
UKHW022313280225
455674UK00004B/294